CHAPTER ONE

CHOICES

Sage, dark, cloaked in black, mysterious,
stands in front of her,
Alisa Fare,
begging for a reaction.
He watches her intently with a smug look on his face.
They face each other in anticipation of what's going to come next.

SAGE
(smirking)
You have a choice.

ALISA
Do I, Sage? Do I really have a choice? You've been making all the decisions for me, and now you expect me to start making decisions?
(thinking)
You've crippled me...You've damaged me.

Suddenly, there is a quick flash of light as
Sage lifts his hand,
to run his finger over her lips.
She holds her face in agony to look up at Sage.
Her cheeks redden.

SAGE
How dare you.

ALISA
Look at me, look at what you did.

She drops her hand and Sage notices the blood forming in the center of her bottom lip.

The blood drips in time for Sage to
catch it on his fingertip.

He places his finger in his own mouth
Intense-

SAGE

I won't be making your decisions any longer.

ALISA

(tearing up, confused)

What do you expect me to do?

SAGE

Choose.

She stands there
confused,
isolated,
hurt.

He begins to leave walking past her,
Until he stops at the door,
hesitating a moment.

SAGE

There is a Glazestar in the top drawer. You are going to need it.

She can feel her eyes enlarge and the anger flooding through her veins
As he walks out the door leaving her,
alone.

CHAPTER TWO

NEW HOPE

Alisa watches as Sage walks into the bright outdoors. He stops for a moment, rubbing his head, wondering if he made the right decision and if he should come back.

At least, that's what she hopes.
A Glazestar, Sage said...

She walks over to the black dresser placed in the center of the room.

She pulls out a liquid filled engraved blade with a gold tip and her mind takes her back to her childhood.

She sees her father,
Tim Fare,

He's aged, staring at the same blade
He looks away, and Alisa sees Sage picking up the blade and pointing it toward her father's head.

ALISA
No!

A loud crashing sound is heard coming from outside. She comes back to reality.

She swings open the door to check on the noise.

ALISA

SAGE! Sage?!

There is nothing going on outside, except for the eerie rustle of the leaves until a piercing screech makes her grab her ears in pain.

A huge demonic creature with a white face jumps down *from the trees outside her home and tries to attack.*

The Screechers are back.

She gets away just in time, slamming the door in their face.

ALISA

No ... I thought we were past this.

An old man wearing a white lab coat approaches the door. It is Dr. Haggard, white haired and aged.

DR. HAGGARD

Alisa, we know that you are in there; we don't mean you any harm. We just want to talk.

She looks through the crack in the blinds until she spots him. He is dark and mysterious.

She watches him for a moment until his eyes meet her eyes through the cracks.

He talks directly to her.

DR. HAGGARD

(grinning)

I repeat, we mean you no harm, but we will use force.

She makes a quick dash to the living room.

There has to be an escape.

But where?

Her eyes catch an open window toward the back of the kitchen.

She runs as fast as she can but a notebook laying on the countertop attracts her attention.

She grabs it on the way out.

Dr. Haggard nods his head and the door blows open.

He steps in, sending in the Screechers to tear through the house.

However, Alisa has managed to escape.

Dr. Haggard picks up a picture of Alisa and slowly slides his finger down the slick glass plate over her face.

Close, but not close enough.

She runs through an abandoned neighborhood, breathing heavily until she gets to a crossroad.
Panting, she looks around.
The city is desolate, expanding on and on in all directions.
She bolts down the road, pulling out her cellphone, to call the only person she trusts.
Robin. She will know what to do.
However, she only gets Robin's voicemail.

ALISA
(frantic)
Robin...Robin answer...please...Robin, listen to me, Sage is gone…he's going after him...we have to hurry...I did all I could.

Robin, sweet yet serious,
is Alisa's only friend, but she's also left her alone.
She throws her phone hard against the ground and it bursts open.
Frustrated, she continues running until she notices a car parked down an abandoned alley.
She opens the gas cap and grabs the keys inside to turn on the car.
She's seen this place before, somewhere in her many dreams.
Alisa takes a deep breath while turning on the car.
What has happened?
Has Sage really left her?
Her thoughts run wild, rampaging in her mind.
She lays her head on the steering wheel and tries to hold in the tears that start welling up in her eyes.

ALISA
(bangs fist on wheel)

Sage!

She looks up to the rear view mirror and Sage appears for a moment.

She quickly checks another mirror but he is no longer there. She knows he's somewhere watching her,

She can feel him.

Somewhere.

CHAPTER THREE

THE LAB

Robin bursts through Fare Corps' research lab and everyone stops their work and stares at her.

She walks over to a naked Alisa floating in a tank full of a dark blue liquid.

Her body is flinching and everyone is watching in anticipation.

The monitors are all going off in alarm.

ETHAN

You knew what this would mean.

ROBIN

She still has time.

ETHAN

She's in too deep now.

ROBIN

She knows what she's doing.

ETHAN

It's only been a few hours since we injected her with the Virus. It's taking over her brain too rapidly.

ROBIN

She just needs a little more time.

ETHAN

You're the only one authorized to pull the plug. Just know that the longer you wait...we won't be able to pull her out. And we can't afford to lose her...

ROBIN

We won't lose her.

Alisa floats in a tube of water with wires running throughout her body.

Robin shakes her head, unsure of her fate.

CHAPTER FOUR

REVERIE

Alisa presses the gas pedal harder as she speeds through the city, in no particular direction.

Her eyes dart to the notebook on the seat beside her, so she quickly opens it to look around for any clues.

A map falls out onto her. She quickly grabs it and she reveals it to show a huge red X in the middle of the city.

She accelerates her speed even more, and her car flies through the empty streets of an abandoned place.

Alisa pulls up to a park to where she thinks the X will be, and she gets out of the car.

She looks around and there are people, frozen, as if they are frozen in time.

Eerie.

She passes by a few people and she can't understand what she is seeing.

She nears the center of Central Park and she sees a young girl with black hair dressed in all black with pale skin.

The young girl stands with her arm extended to Alisa.

MORBID-

ALISA

Hey! Hey, please, can you hear me?

Her eyes are hidden from Alisa.

YOUNG GIRL

Don't be afraid, Alisa.

ALISA

I need help.

YOUNG GIRL

What is it you seek?

ALISA

Sage.

The young girl begins to step away.
She lowers her arm and there is a darker essence in the air.
Haunted—

YOUNG GIRL

You do not need to seek Sage; you need to seek to find what's left of yourself. Do you even know who you are, Alisa?

ALISA

That doesn't matter.

YOUNG GIRL

Then you will remain here indefinitely.

ALISA

What...

(looking around)

Where am I?!

YOUNG GIRL

(voice grows demonic)

What's wrong Alisa? Things don't seem as real to you anymore?

The young girl turns very dark and sinister.
Alisa takes out the Glazestar and strikes the young girl.
However, the girl gives a crooked smile and disappears in a cloud of dark air.
She leaves behind a storm of falling photos.
Alisa picks up some of the pictures to take a closer look.

She sees herself as child, holding files of notes of some of the procedures that had been done to her.

There's screaming in the air as she rummages through them. Alisa feels sick as she sees flashes in her mind.

Flashes of
underwater,
needles,
blood,
surgical instruments,
defibrillators.

Alisa's eyes are drawn to her wrists and her veins. Marks begin to show up, slowly painting deep lines down her arms.

ALISA

Leave me alone!

WOMAN

Excuse me?

A stalky woman is standing in front of her. The frozen people are now unfrozen and busily rushing to get to their next destination

ALISA

I'm sorry.

Alisa notices the Glazestar, which is still in her hand. She quickly tucks it behind her and makes her way back to the car.

On the way there, Jeff Neal, sophisticated, young, and handsome spots Alisa and stops her.

JEFF

Alisa, hey, hey, how's it going?

ALISA

Not now...I'm busy.

JEFF
(offended)
Whoa, whoa...sorry, I just thought...

ALISA
Where did my car go? I swear I parked my car right here...

JEFF
Alisa...are you ok?

ALISA
Yes...

(pause)

I'm fine.

JEFF
I'm sorry...yea, this might be a bad time...

ALISA
How do you know me?

JEFF
(confused)
The Ward...

ALISA
(under her breath)
The Ward?

JEFF
Yea? With the others. We go there all the time.

ALISA
I don't know, I'm sorry...I need rest...

JEFF
I can take you back to your place if you want?

ALISA
(thinking)
Right...I don't want to go there right now...

JEFF
We can go back to my place...

ALISA
(her eyes search his)
We've been there before, haven't we?

JEFF
A few times.

ALISA
(cautious, looking around)
Let's go.

Alisa follows Jeff at an awfully long distance, hoping that somehow she will feel Sage's presence.
And hoping that the sophisticated, handsome guy is someone who she could trust in this lonely town.

CHAPTER FIVE

JEFF'S RESIDENCE

Jeff places a cup of tea in front of Alisa and she eagerly takes it and sips it.

She inhales the reality of the tea and sulks.

The room is warm, aligned with different oblong picture frames on the walls of droopy clocks and little mice.

Did he live there all by himself?

She shutters at that thought; no one should ever have to be alone.

The loneliness in the air clung to the walls and passes her whenever a breeze comes.

Jeff clears his throat.

JEFF

How are you feeling?

ALISA

Afraid.

JEFF

Still having visions of this "Sage" thing?

Alisa's eyes widen and she nearly coughs on her next sip of the tea. She stands, and it alerts Jeff.

JEFF

Hey, hey, hey, calm down...sorry...we don't have to mention that name...

ALISA

Sage, I told you about Sage?

JEFF

Yes, many times...he's just a figment of your imagination. Someone who disturbs you sometimes—he's not real and he can't hurt you.

ALISA

Not real?

JEFF

Not real.

(pause)

Have you been to see Dr. Haggard lately?

Alisa walks over to the blinds, and she peeks out the window to see if anyone is watching her.

ALISA

Dr. Haggard...my...

JEFF

Shrink...

ALISA

Yes...I remember now, no—I haven't seen him in a while—I don't think I want to keep seeing him.

JEFF

Aw, too bad, he was really starting to get to you.

ALISA

Exactly why it was a good time to stop...

JEFF

Alisa, please...talk to me...it's been a week, what's going on?

Alisa looks into his bright green eyes.

She pauses for a moment and realizes there is some genuine care in Jeff's concern for her.

ALISA

What is this?

JEFF

Alisa...I...

ALISA

Why can't I remember anything?...

JEFF

Why does this seem to surprise you? You left me...just like that...no words or explanations...you just took off...and I thought I'd never see you again...

ALISA

Jeff, I can't explain it, but Sage...I saw him...he came to me...he gave me this.

(reveals the Glazestar)

JEFF

(shocked)

Hey, what are you doing with that?

ALISA

Listen to me, I have to stop him before it's too late—before he kills my father.

JEFF

Alisa...you're doing it again...you said the very same thing before you left me...I can't have you do this to me again...you need help...

ALISA

What are you talking about?

JEFF

I just think you need to get some help, I care about you, I want you to get better…

ALISA

What are you doing? What's going on?

JEFF

Alisa, give me the Glazestar...

Alisa hears a door opening from the other room and she begins to panic.

Jeff lunges for the Glazestar and knocks her off guard. The Glazestar is knocked away underneath the dining table. Alisa makes a run for an exit but she quickly realizes she is trapped.

Dr. Haggard walks into the room and she falls to the ground, struggling, as the Screechers restrain her.

CHAPTER SIX

THE WARD

Alisa wakes up in a white room, in a straightjacket strapped to a chair.

Dr. Haggard sits before her.

DR. FARE
(voice)
Ah, Alisa, it's time to wake up.

ALISA
Daddy?

Oh no!
Her eyes clear to focus on Dr. Haggard, she struggles in her chair.

ALISA
Dr. Haggard...please...

DR. HAGGARD
It's been a while. Alisa, how are you feeling?

Alisa shakes her head, looking around the room for an escape.

DR. HAGGARD
Any more little visits from Sage?

ALISA
No...he left me.

DR. HAGGARD
He's left you? Where did he go?

ALISA

I don't know...

DR. HAGGARD

Alisa, it's ok, you can trust me.

ALISA

He didn't tell me, I'm on my own now.

DR. HAGGARD

You were always on your own, Alisa.

ALISA

I'm not crazy, Dr. Haggard. You have to believe me; he is your real enemy.

DR. HAGGARD

Is that so?

ALISA

When will you let me go?

DR. HAGGARD

I'm afraid that's not possible Alisa...

ALISA

I don't understand, I haven't done anything wrong!

DR. HAGGARD

I don't think you can manage the real world without assistance. You are a danger not only to yourself, but to others.

ALISA

(repeating)

I haven’t done anything wrong.

DR. HAGGARD

Alisa, there isn't a person named Sage, to any of our knowledge. He only exists in your head. This shows to me you are incapable of knowing your true reality. We need to get you better.

ALISA

No, I'm not crazy, I know what's real and what's not...this is a huge misunderstanding. Jeff will tell you...I'm not crazy!

DR. HAGGARD

Don't worry Alisa, you won't be fighting your demons alone anymore. We want to help you get better.

Dr. Haggard stands up and begins to walk toward the exit. Alisa begins to freak out and struggle harder against her restraints.

ALISA

Wait...where are you going? You can't leave me here...please...please... don't do this. Jeff? Jeff!

Behind a two-way glass mirror awaits Jeff, watching, with tearstained eyes.

JEFF

She will get better right?

DR. HAGGARD

She will need some work, but I have seen progress.

JEFF

Yea, I hope so Dr. Haggard...I can't bear to see her like this.

DR. HAGGARD

Don't worry, we will take good care of her. Go home, get some rest. We'll keep you in touch.

JEFF

Thank you again.

Jeff watches as Alisa begins to break down, begging and pleading to get out but there is nothing that he can do.

He grows so uncomfortable that he leaves the room, unable to watch any further.

Alisa is back in a cold dark room, sitting on her bed staring into space.

A nurse comes in to give her food along with a small cup of medicine, but Alisa doesn't move.

NURSE

You have to eat; if you don't, we'll use force.

ALISA

I'm not hungry.

NURSE

I will leave this here for you, and if I get back and it's still here, you will be eating your food through a tube.

The nurse leaves and Alisa still doesn't move.

She lays down on the bed in fetal position.

ALISA

Look at what you've done to me. You're not even real.

Alisa lays in defeat until she hears footsteps by the door.

The door opens, and she turns around ready to fight back.

ALISA

Go ahead and put it in!

SAGE

Are you giving up already? You're pathetic.

ALISA
(startled)

Go away!

SAGE

Come on Alisa, don't be like that...I thought we got past that?

ALISA

No, I can't do this anymore, I'm done with you.

SAGE

I thought you were going to stop me?

ALISA

Look at where you've gotten me.

SAGE

Ah, come on, The Ward? That's what it takes to stop you?

ALISA

They will never let me out of here...

SAGE

I beg to differ...the door is wide open...let me prove it to you.

Sage holds out his hand and waits for Alisa to take it. She hesitates but realizes she will not be able to get out without help.

With a deep breath, Alisa takes his hand and all fades to black.

ALISA
(disoriented)

What did you do to me?

SAGE

Shhh, listen to what you told me...

Alisa is lying in New York City's Central Park having a picnic with Sage. He is a bit awkward, fumbling to open a plastic container, but Alisa is making him feel special by presenting him with dozens of dandelions.

She lays them on his legs and around his body while she hums a sweet melody.

Her white gown flows in the gentle wind as she rises up to pick out another dandelion.

She places it inside a small jar and holds it out to Sage.

ALISA

Here, this is for you.

SAGE

I don't understand.

ALISA

It's a dandelion, you can't waste this on just anything though; use it only when you absolutely have to...

SAGE

What do I do with it?

ALISA

You can make a wish, silly, any wish you like...just take it out and blow it into the world...and may all your dreams come true.

SAGE

And you so freely give me my first wish?

ALISA

Yes, everyone deserves at least one wish.

SAGE

You're beautiful, Alisa. I never knew such a thing existed.

ALISA

Well, you do now, so make it count.

SAGE

I'm afraid I have nothing to give back to you.

ALISA

Sage, I don't need anything in return...your presence is enough for me.

SAGE

Is there another like you here?

ALISA

What do you mean?

SAGE

Another being like you?

ALISA

(laughs)

I don't understand.

SAGE

I didn't think so. You're a rare find and that's such a shame.

Sage looks at Alisa, who still is a bit lost at his words.
He watches her lay back, allowing the sunlight to light her face.
The dandelion crumbles along with the world around them.

Alisa awakes from her slumber to see citizens passing by her, as if unnoticed by the blinded society.
Her eyes are red and she still is in her white Ward attire.
She gets herself to her feet and looks around in confusion.

After a few blocks of walking, she finds her car back in the same alley.

Deja-Vu.

A phone ring startles her.

She follows the sound inside the car to the dashboard. It continues to chime as she reads the caller ID.

It's Sarah.

She misses the call and the voicemail flashes on the screen. She plays the message while she climbs into the driver's seat.

SARAH (V.O)

Hey sis, long time no talk. I got a phone call from Jeff. He seemed pretty freaked out, told me you were in the Ward...I'm not going to lie to you, it's freaking me out. Listen, I know I haven't been the best sister lately, I've had a lot of stuff going on...the Ailment, the kids, Reevie...but hey, I want to let you know I'm still here for you if you need me. I love you, I hope you know that. So, stop being so stubborn...just accept the help...we know you will get through this. Sage—Sage is a nightmare and he will ruin your life. He ruined our familys' life…I'm not going to let him ruin yours. Take care, Ally.

Alisa is unsettled as she hangs up the phone.

Her car dings, alerting her that she's running out of gas, so she pulls up to a nearby gas station.

She deletes the voicemail and then gets out the car to head into the store.

She looks around the corner for the attendant.

Ethan appears from the back and presents himself when Alisa's head is turned.

He is odd, staring into her eyes, yet not looking at her.

Alisa reaches into her pocket and pulls out a Chip.

ALISA

(looking toward pump)

Uhm, I guess use whatever's left on pump 8...regular gas...

ETHAN

Alisa, is that you?

Alisa looks up to realize that the attendant looks familiar, so she looks at his nametag to remember his name.

She exhales and laughs.

ALISA

(confused)

Ethan?

ETHAN

It's been a long time, how are you feeling?

ALISA

I'm feeling ok...why? Why would I not be ok?

ETHAN

Well, you disappeared on us for a while...no one knew what happened to you. You just didn't seem to be feeling well.

ALISA

No, no. I'm feeling fine. Great actually.

ETHAN

Well, hey, that's great to hear. How's Jeff doing?

ALISA

He's doing fine, but I'm not so sure about him.

ETHAN

That's too bad...I really thought you found yourself a good one.

(pause)

Well, it was really good to see you, keep that pretty smile on your face...we need something in this eerie town...

Alisa nods and walks back out to her car to pump the gas. While she waits patiently for the gas to fill up she notices a flyer sticking from outside her window.

She grabs the flyer and her eyes catch a photo of a group of people sitting around in a circle.

In bold print, the words say "Self-Help Group Therapy." She looks closer at the faces in the group and notices that Sage is siting amongst them.

The pump clicks off, startling her back to reality. She quickly hangs up the nozzle and drives off.

Alisa travels down a long flat road until she gets to the address listed on the paper.

There is a meeting already in session when Alisa walks through the doors.

She maneuvers her way to the back of the auditorium, hoping not to draw attention to herself.

Once she finds a seat, she observes, in expectation of answers.

GUY

I lost my way, I felt like the only thing I could think about was to use. It became my life, it consumed me. But here I found hope, I found love, I found life. Thanks.

Next, Jeff approaches the stand. Alisa ducks lower in her seat so that he doesn't see her.

JEFF

Hello everyone, my name is Jeff Neal. I am in mourning for the loss of my girlfriend. The love of my life. Alisa Fare. Alisa Fare was not like any ordinary girl. I actually met her here in group therapy. Many of you may know her. She really helped me to get over my depression. She taught me to love my life and the people in it. Alisa, was such a strong woman on the outside, she could take down anything that came in her way. But, when it came to her own mind, she became a victim to her own demons. They consumed her, well, he consumed her. Sage. He was the real enemy.

Alisa touches her cheeks to feel tears rushing down them. She stands to her feet and sneaks out toward the back, still invisible to those around her.

As she travels through the halls of the auditorium, she covers her ears to block Jeff's speech, but it still manages to pierce her ears.

JEFF

It's amazing to see how much our minds can trick us into believing in another reality. Alisa never talked about her past, or her future. She stayed in the present...I'm just not sure what present that was in her mind. Her goal became to get to know Sage, wait till he was vulnerable, then destroy him. She went on about viruses and how she would be saving the World. I just let her talk...hoping one day she would realize there was no "virus" out to get us...we didn't need a "cure". But she was long gone. She doesn't even know where she came from...But I loved her and I believed her. And I feel like I've betrayed my best friend. I pray she gets better, like she helped me get better. Thanks.

Alisa begins to run down the hall and then finally out the doors into a bright light.

CHAPTER SEVEN

THE POD

Alisa bursts into another hallway of a new building with testing materials and scientists scattered around working on various projects.

As she walks through the room no one seems to be able to see her.

Some scientists are working on computers while others are discussing specimens and antidotes.

A few wild animals are locked up in cages going mad as they shriek at her, consisting of small monkeys, rodents, and small dogs.

The whispers continue as the scientists look through microscopes and try to contain the animals.

She follows the action to the next room in the direction of the chaos.

SCIENTIST

All her labs are looking normal.

LAB ASSISTANT

She's just had an episode from the Illness. All we can do is wait and keep her hydrated.

Alisa tries to get a look at what they are hovering over. Her eyes widen with fear once she notices that it's her body!

ROBIN

Alisa, you have to focus right now, I know you can hear me.

Alisa hears Robin's voice echoing around her. She looks around for the source because it echoes across her World in many directions.

ALISA

Robin?

Alisa approaches her floating body inside a huge container of dark blue liquid. She puts her hand on the glass and shakes her head in incertitude.

ALISA

What are you doing to me?

ROBIN

Alisa, Alisa? What's going on, why is she doing that?

Alisa watches herself as she opens her eyes in the container and starts to thrash around.

She feels her World start to slip as she steadies herself on a nearby wall.

ROBIN

Code 7, Code 7! Hurry, someone give her sedative, now! Shh, Alisa look at me, look at me for a second.

Alisa in the container is staring at herself on the floor, who is now holding onto her head going in and out of consciousness.

ROBIN

Yea, there we go, you're going to be ok, hang in there...You'll be ok...It's Robin, You're Alisa, we need to find Sage. You have to stay in that world. I can't pull you out...You're going to be ok...Remember you have to......

There is a long eerie pause as Alisa finds herself being sedated back into her coma state.

Alisa is sucked back out into a white light and into a soft bed. A figure is above her rubbing her hair.

A light shines on the figure's face revealing Dr. Fare, and a Young Alisa.

DR. FARE

Remember, you have to realize that I love you, and I would never leave you...I'm just sick darling...but daddy will get better soon...You will make us all better one day, sweetie.

YOUNG ALISA

I'll be a scientist, like you daddy.

DR. FARE

Of course you will be baby; try to get some sleep.

YOUNG ALISA

I love you.

DR. FARE

I love you more than you will ever know...

Dr. Fare gets up, leaving young Alisa by herself in the dark room to go to sleep.

Moments later-

Alisa tosses and turns in bed but she can't seem to get to sleep.

She hears a commotion coming from down the stairs, so she gets out of bed.

She travels down the stairs to find her father pacing around in the living room, rubbing his head with one hand.

In his other hand he holds the Glazestar; he puts it to his head and takes it away.

Young Alisa stands there, watching in silence and seeing that her father is very distraught.

Sage stands in between the two as Dr. Fare
puts the Glazestar to his head.

Silence falls as Alisa yells,

Daddy!

ALISA

Daddy!

Alisa's eyes snap open and she pops out of Jeff's arms. She stares into the darkness until Jeff pulls her to him.

JEFF

Hey, hey, hey, it's ok, it was just a dream.

Jeff switches on a light and Alisa quickly grabs for a cup of water sitting beside her on the counter.

She inhales deeply as she takes a big gulp.

ALISA

I don't know what's real anymore.

JEFF

Baby, I'm here. I'm real.

She takes a look around the room and her eyes catch the gigantic ceilings and the large empty space between the bed and the exit.

Alisa is in satin nightwear while Jeff is in torn jeans and a plain shirt. She turns to search his eyes but all she can see is his concern.

Had he fallen asleep with her?

Yes, he had.

The way he touched her, it was as if he had always touched her.

Why couldn't she remember anything that happened between the two of them?

She ignores the thoughts that come cascading in her mind. She knows she can trust him, he has those kind of eyes.

However, she still has questions that need answers and she needs them now.

ALISA

Jeff, you put me in the the Ward...you told me I needed to get help.

JEFF

(uncertain)

Ally...I'm just starting to get to know you...It's only been a few weeks...I think you're a cool chick and all....

ALISA

You don't know me?

JEFF

I know you, just not very well...yet...

Alisa takes a deep breath and pulls herself out of the king size bed they share.

Jeff stares at her for a moment until he finally sputters out the words.

JEFF

Something I said? Are you leaving?

ALISA

No... I just need more water...

JEFF

Ok...

Alisa makes her way to the kitchen and pours more water into her glass.

She sits at the counter and rubs her head.

The kitchen is similar to the kitchen in her childhood.

She looks at the hallway of where she would have been in the dream.

Then the voices start.

Her eyes cut to Sage, who is watching her in the corner of the room.

A small version of herself stands near him, crying.

YOUNG ALISA
(sobbing)
Daddy, Daddy! No! Daddy, why!

ALISA
He's not after my father...

Sage moves from the shadows and into view.

Alisa sits quietly shaking her head.

SAGE
He was weak.

ALISA
He was Sick.

SAGE
They are all Sick.

ALISA
What's real, Sage? Is this what you wanted me to choose? What do you want from me?

SAGE
You came to me.

Alisa looks at Sage, and for the first time she sees an old friend in him.

She tries to think for a moment but her heart starts to race.

She grabs her head and feels nauseous.

ALISA
(remembering)
I want us to go back to how we used to be...before all this...

SAGE
It's not the same anymore, Alisa.

ALISA
What are you saying?

Sage approaches Alisa and touches her face.
He peers into her eyes, making Alisa freeze.
This is the first time Sage has shown sympathy to her.
SUDDENLY: It all comes back to her now.
Her eyes widen, and the mission is back on.
Faint whispers begin to play all around her.
She closes her eyes and Sage leans in to kiss her until the whispers get louder.

ROBIN (V.O)
Remember—you have to kill Sage.

Alisa opens her eyes and pulls away before he can kiss her.

SAGE
Alisa?

ALISA
Sorry, Jeff is waiting for me upstairs...I have to go.

Sage watches her leave before stepping back into the shadows.
Alisa finds her way back into the bedroom and crawls into the oversize bed with Jeff.
He wraps his arms around her and she stares at a picture of Jeff and herself.

ALISA
(whisper)
This isn't real. I'm dreaming.

She finally closes her eyes to remember:
Scientists gathering around outside a bright white room, observing Alisa.

She only has a thin white sheet wrapped around her body that they called a gown.

The slow walk up the vault of water kept Alisa's mind still. All she can focus on is whether the water is as cold as the floor she had slept on for most of her life.

She centers herself inside the Pod, allowing the water to rise up her body.

Robin and a few other scientists step into the room with needles in their hands.

ROBIN
Hello Alisa, how are you feeling today?

ALISA
Excellent, never felt better.

ROBIN
Today's the day. You've trained well and your body is magnificent. Are you ready for the final injection?

ALISA
Yes.

ROBIN
This last shot will activate the virus that is being suppressed inside you.

ALISA

I'm ready...

ROBIN
(pause, sincere)
You're very brave, Alisa.

ALISA
I have to complete my father's work.

Robin nods.
She picks up a needle from one of her assistants and carefully guides the sharp point into Alisa's soft flesh.

Alisa closes her eyes as her blood trickles from another line back into the vein of the Pod's chamber.

Robin submerges Alisa into the water and locks the vault.

Alisa holds her breath as she watches Robin move to the IV pole to begin the transfusion.

The tubes release the poison back into her veins and the Virus is activated.

Robin can't take her eyes off Alisa; she places her hand on the transparent glass as Alisa slowly loses the fight to keep her eyes open. Alisa fades into the blackness.

ROBIN
Welcome to Reverie.

CHAPTER EIGHT

REVERIE

Alisa stands in the middle of a busy, anonymous city with people walking fast all around her.

Even though there are people around her, she stills feels a sense of loneliness.

She gets to a crossroad and notices there are some citizens who are frozen.

Sage walks between the people, looking at them and touching their frozen bodies.

A gasp escapes her mouth, alerting Sage.
They make eye contact.

SAGE

Ah-lis-ah...

ALISA

You know my name?

SAGE

I know Alisa.

ALISA

You don't belong here.

SAGE
(he tilts his head)

You don't belong here.

ALISA

Sage, don't.

Sage begins to darken and his arms begin to shift into piercing blades.

His eyes redden and he charges to Alisa until sirens sound. A few black and white cars show up with a golden emblem on the side.

A few officers rush to Alisa's defense, managing to fire bullets into Sage but they pass right through him

He smiles in return before making an escape as more police officers approach them.

A suave Officer makes his way up to the front to greet Alisa.

OFFICER

It's ok Ma'am, he won't get too far.

ALISA

Sage…I…I'm ok.

Alisa holds her head and tries to make sense of this new world she's in.

She looks at the Captain, who is wearing dark sunglasses so she can't see his eyes.

Cool. Obscure.

ALISA

Thank you sir, I know he won't.

OFFICER

We don't want you out here getting hurt, let's get you somewhere safe.

ALISA

No, no, no, I can't...I have to be out here...I have to be near Sage, learn about him...his next moves...I appreciate you guys stepping in. Thank you.

OFFICER

Excuse me?

ALISA

I'm on a mission...I can't forget that...I have to go find him.

The Officer watches her as she walks away, not taking his eyes off her until she turns a corner.

OFFICER

(to himself)

This is where we've come to.

(to others)

Alright guys, fix it up.

Alisa navigates through the crowd of frozen and unfrozen oblivious people.

She realizes a trail is forming from the icy citizens as she follows them. It has to lead to where Sage is.

After a following the trail for a few blocks she ends up standing in front of a familiar place.

It's her home.

She walks cautiously up the stairs leading to her front door.

She tries the door and realizes it's open, so she goes in.

The front door takes her right inside to the kitchen area.

Everything is just as she had left it as a little girl.

Bare walls, gigantic clocks hanging all over the house, and the same exact placement of the emerald DNA structure centered in the middle of the dining room.

She traces her fingers over the smooth edges until she hears whispers coming from the TV room.

REPORTER

It's tragic news here in Times Square. Millions of people are infected and dying each day from the Severe Acute Genetic Epidemic. It seems like the conditions just keep getting worse and worse. We are losing the battle... (coughing harshly).

The reporter is standing near Times Square looking at all the people scattered around the streets, but especially toward the hospitals.

There are some shops with broken windows and debris left in the streets.

REPORTER

It has been rumored that the leak of the Virus came from the root of our most prestigious research facility, FARE CORPS. Our city is in desperate need. Schools have been closed down, roads are blocked. The whole city is being shut down and evacuated. If you have any flulike symptoms, it's best to get to your nearest hospital immediately. Otherwise, stay indoors and wear masks till you can get out of the city to prevent further spread of the Virus. This is Amanda Reguer reporting from MED Breaking News.

The reporter tries to handle the chaos but she finds herself coughing and losing her train of thought.

People are in panic around the city, trying to leave and trying to get in and out the hospitals.

People are wearing face masks, and are stuck in their cars trying to evacuate the city.

Some citizens have completely lost their minds.
A few people are walking around in a demented state of consciousness.

Toward the middle of the city a tall building stands, surrounded by groups of people.

Fare Corps.
Robin and her team look over the city to all the people outside going insane.

After injecting Alisa with the Virus, they gather outside Alisa's room by a window trying to figure out how they can buy more time.

She shakes her head as she watches the deranged crowd outside her doors.

A few people are banging on the building, trying to get in because they heard that there may be some sort of treatment for them. They are chanting, "Give us the cure!"

Lacey and Ethan stand by watching through the window with Robin.,

ROBIN

They won't stop. They know.

LACEY

This place has a way of leaking. I'm surprised we aren't all under water by now.

ROBIN

She's our only hope of survival.

(pause)

We're coming to the end.

ETHAN

No, Dr. Leighman. It will work, this is only the beginning.

Robin pats Ethan's shoulder and walks away, leaving Ethan and Lacey to watch over the citizens desperately trying to enter the building.

LACEY

You can't trust her. She's going to drown all of us.

ETHAN

Lacey, what you're suggesting is absurd. Now is not the time to start pulling against each other, we need to work together.

LACEY

How can you work with someone who is ready and willing to slit your throat for their own personal gain? I warned you, Ethan. Watch your back.

Lacey walks off in the opposite direction of Robin while Ethan continues to watch as he coughs silently.

CHAPTER NINE

SAGE

Sage is enamored with the TV.
He stands in silence, drinking in the action.
Does he enjoy watching the Virus spread?
Or is he hurt by his own doing?
Alisa draws closer to him, yet Sage is not startled by her.
He is expecting her.

SAGE

Sage?

ALISA

Yes.

SAGE

What is Sage?

ALISA

It's what we call—you are.

SAGE

And you are Alisa?

ALISA

Yes.

SAGE

All those people, what's happening to them?

ALISA

They are dying.

SAGE

Dying?

(pause)

Am I dying?

ALISA

No.

(quietly)

Sage, you can't be here...This is my body, my mind.

Sage slowly starts to grow and his hands begin to blacken. Alisa watches as his eyes darken.

SAGE

I think you should go. This is my home now.

Alisa quickly dodges out the way as Sage attacks her. He cuts through some of the kitchen's wall and whatever he touches it disintegrates in front of Alisa.

Alisa runs to the other room to look for any type of weapon to protect her.

She picks up a few picture frames and items on the coffee table and throws them at Sage.

But he is unstoppable.

Alisa tries her best to keep her distance until he finally reaches her and picks her up by her neck.

ALISA

(sputtering)

Sage, please...I'm sorry.

Sage stares at her for a moment. Alisa's heartbeat intensifies, and Sage can hear it through her shirt.

He suddenly drops her down to the ground and backs up. Alisa grabs her neck and starts coughing.

ALISA

Why did you let me go?

SAGE

There's something in there.

Alisa feels her chest but there's nothing coming from that specific area.

The heartbeat echoes throughout the whole room and she looks around everywhere..

ALISA

It's my heart.

SAGE

Heart?

ALISA

I have a heart. It pumps blood throughout my whole body. I can't live without my heart.

SAGE

Heart.

Sage feels for his heart.

ALISA

We're different in that way Sage, you don't have a heart.

SAGE

I want a heart.

ALISA

(thinking)

I'll help you find one, we just need to get a better understanding of each other, that's all.

Sage nods his head.
Alisa walks around the room and sees what they destroyed.
She picks up a picture frame and notices it's a picture of her father and her as a child.
She sets it upright and then she smiles at Sage, who gives her a blank stare.

ALISA
(looking around)
Where are we, Sage?

Alisa and Sage walk outside to the city before them.
It's an eerie place, with only a few people on the streets.
Alisa and Sage walk around and view the odd world but also realize how beautiful and mystical it is.

ALISA
(breathless)
This is how I imagine the world.

Alisa walks over and checks out a large white oak tree that sticks out in the middle of nowhere.
She is mesmerized by it.
She sees there is fruit budding on the tree and after she plucks a fruit, she smells it.
She attempts to bite into the fruit until she turns around to hear someone yelling at her.

OLD MAN
Hey, hey, what are you doing? I hope you plan on buying that. Nothing's free here.

ALISA

I'm sorry... I....

The tree and Sage are no longer there.
She searches around for Sage but all she sees is this old man hounding her.

OLD MAN
Well, what's it going to be, pay up!

ALISA
(checks pocket)
I don't have any money, I'm sorry...

JEFF
Hey, it's no problem, I got it.

ALISA
Thank you...

JEFF
No worries. Apple a day keeps the doctor away, isn't that right old man?

OLD MAN
Yea, yea.

Jeff winks at Alisa and then head off toward the auditorium she saw earlier.
Interested, she follows Jeff.

Alisa walks into the building and notices there are a few people already seated.
They all are in a circle.
Alisa is spotted immediately and one seat is left unattended.

GROUP LEADER
Welcome, we have a new face everyone. Please come and join us.

Alisa slowly walks over to take a seat. She is hesitant, but when she sits she sees that Sage is also sitting in the circle across from her.

GROUP LEADER

Would you like to tell the group your name and why you've come to join us?

ALISA

Uh, well, I'm Alisa...

GROUP

Hello Alisa.

ALISA

And I'm not quite sure what I'm here for...

There is a bit of chatter and some whispers.

GROUP LEADER

Ah, come on Alisa, it's ok, you're in a safe environment, what is talked about in group therapy stays in group therapy. It's our privacy policy. So please, don't be afraid.

ALISA

I, uhm, well...

JEFF

Maybe she's not quite ready to confront her issues right now...It took me a while...after I lost myself due to that illness. I thought I was going insane. It does help though, to open up and be honest about how you feel, it's a nice release. We're all here to help one another.

ALISA

(to Sage)

I don't understand...why you brought me here.

SAGE

You said you want to better understand each other.

ALISA

Yes, each other, not myself.

The group looks around to each other and then back to Alisa. She is talking to herself.

ALISA

What's wrong?

JEFF

There's no one sitting there.

ALISA

He... was just right there...

GROUP LEADER

Who, Alisa?

ALISA

Sage.

GROUP LEADER

Sage? Who is Sage?

ALISA

He brought me here... I'm sorry, I have to go.

Sage continues to watch Alisa as she storms out the door. She walks down the street in the pitch dark, and the feeling of someone watching her lingers.

A lamppost appears in front of her and the light grows brighter.

ALISA
You made me out to look insane!

SAGE
No I didn't. You did.

ALISA
What are you talking about?

SAGE
Only you can see me.

ALISA
I don't—I don't understand.

SAGE
Ask yourself that question.

ALISA
No, you're real...

SAGE
Are they real?

ALISA
(demanding)
I don't know. Why did you bring me there?

SAGE
I didn't bring you there.

ALISA
Oh no, I have to go back.

SAGE

(looking away)

Love transcends all time, and space. Doesn't it overcome all?

ALISA

No, he's not real.

Alisa notices a gigantic wall with a large letters sketched unto it revealing: "ALISA+JEFF".

He is tormenting her again. What did he want her to see? She quickly rushes through the crowds, getting turned around and lost in the mass of people, but the only face she searching for is Jeff's.

Within a few moments she finds her feet beginning to slow to a stop on a corner by a coffee shop called Moe's.

And there he is, Jeff. Cool. Comforting. He was her comfort.

JEFF

Alisa, hey, hey, how's it going?

ALISA

Jeff!

JEFF

Hey, didn't know you were a fan of coffee, this is one of my favorite coffee shops.

ALISA

Jeff, I'm so sorry I left like that the other night. I was under a lot of pressure and....

JEFF

No need to apologize, hey, this is a crazy idea, but would you like to grab a cup of coffee with me?

ALISA

I...uh...sure, I'd love too.

JEFF

Great, they have all sorts to choose from in this place.

Alisa follows him into the coffee shop and while Jeff orders them coffee she takes a seat by a bright open window.

Her mind wanders, hoping that Jeff will understand, wondering if he can be of any help.

He is all smiles when he takes a seat.

JEFF

I mean, it's so beautiful here, I get lost in this city sometimes. It feels so good to just breathe and take all the sights and smells in. Its peace is like no other.

ALISA

Jeff, it's funny, and it's so weird for me to say, but it feels like we've meet before, like I've known you for a while.

JEFF

People have told me I have an old soul.

ALISA

No, it's not just that...it's like, somehow we're on the same wavelength.

JEFF

Yea, I got that feeling the other night at the group. You're different.

ALISA

Jeff, I know this may be a bit blunt, but I have to know.

JEFF

Ask away.

ALISA

Have we had a conversation before this one?

JEFF
(laughing)
No, I don't believe so?

ALISA
No? You have no idea who I am?

JEFF
Not that I know…of…I mean, that was the first time I saw you at group therapy.

ALISA
This doesn't make any sense. I'm sorry. Jeff, I need to ask you for your help.

JEFF
Yea, sure. What do you need?

ALISA
I need to know, if there is a possibility that you could be real?

JEFF
What?

ALISA
If it were somehow possible that you were actually real, and that this was all a dream for you like it is for me.

JEFF
A dream?

ALISA
Yes, are you real? Is it possible that you're not just a figment of my imagination, but somehow we were in love at one point and now you're here—with me?

JEFF

Alisa, I mean...I don't know what you want me to tell you? What is reality? It's it now, aren't you aware now? Of course I'm real.

ALISA

This isn't funny Jeff. I need to know. I don't know how to talk to the outside world...and I need help... I need to send a message...

JEFF

I don't think you're well.

ALISA

Please, you're probably dreaming right now. I need you to become aware of this moment, ok? Jeff, do you understand? This is critical.

JEFF

Alisa, you're starting to freak me out...

ALISA

Jeff, this isn't real. Look at the world around you. This isn't real...

Alisa tries to pour the coffee out of the coffee mug. Jeff looks at it strangely as the coffee won't come out of the cup.

People start to slow down in the restaurant.

ALISA

I think you are real...and this is your subconscious. I need you to get to Fare Corps and tell my supervisor, Robin Leighman, that I'm fine and I just need a little longer to figure out how I'm going to deal with Sage, ok? Please, I don't know any other way to tell her.

JEFF

I—I'm sorry. I have to go.

ALISA

Jeff, no, wait!

Jeff takes off, running outside the coffee shop and Alisa follows but he disappears into the sea of disconnected people.

CHAPTER TEN

REALITY?

Jeff tosses and turns in his bed.
He shoots up out of his bed as he escapes his nightmare.

After he switches his nightstand light on, he rubs his eyes and tries to make sense of the dream.

He gets a sip of water and pops a few Phase pills.
Then he peeks into the mirror, noting his pale face and his gray eyes.

He coughs into his elbow, trying to suppress himself.
The alarm clock reads 3:12 in the morning.

There is no way he is going to stay up to watch the sun peak over the horizon.

He lays back down and allows himself to fall back into his slumber, but it isn't slumber this time. It is just darkness.

The morning slowly slips by till midday.
Jeff meets with a friend at the Mill, a place where the last remains of food is cooked and shared amongst the community.

On the way he passes by a nearby abandoned coffee shop and a moment of deja vu hits him.

He sees a girl that looks similar to Alisa sitting inside the coffee shop.

As he gets closer he realizes it's not her.
Strange.

From the corner of his eye he spots his friend Brad calling out to him, but he somehow can't shake the unusual experience of the peculiar, brown haired girl.

JEFF

Sorry, I was running a little late. You know how the Givers are, never a dull moment.

BRAD

I get it. Gotta do what you gotta do.

JEFF

Yea. I'm not feeling so well either. I knew it would get to me though. No one's immune.

BRAD

Damn dude, won't be too much longer and all of us are going to be dead.

JEFF

Or crazy. That's why I have to keep working, preventing delusion as long as possible. We've made some progress. We just don't know what to do when they get past Phase 4.

BRAD

No consciousness past Phase 4, huh?

JEFF

None.

BRAD

What stage are you my friend?

JEFF

Phase 2.

BRAD

Well, that's much better than the rest of us, good genes. What's that—extreme fatigue, coughing, chills?

JEFF

Pretty much. My genes aren't good enough. Anyway, I've been having these strange dreams lately. I've been in this weird place. It's a beautiful world...but, there's this girl...I keep seeing her face. I didn't think anything about it until last night.

BRAD

What happened last night?

JEFF

We were at a place very similar to that coffee shop. I mean exactly the same. We were sitting down right over there, and she asked me...I can't...quite...remember.

Brad lifts up his canteen and on the label it says: SO GOOD YOU CAN'T BELIEVE IT'S REAL.

It hits Jeff.

JEFF

She asked me if I was real.

BRAD

(laughing)

Oh yea?

JEFF

Yea, but that's not what bothered me. She began to talk to me, about a lab and a woman named Robin. And something about the S.A.G.E outbreak—I don't know. It seemed so real...like it was a message or something.

BRAD

Yea dude, sounds pretty trippy. What kind of drugs do they have you on?

JEFF

Yea, I don't know...I can't get her out of my head now... like there is something I have to do...

BRAD

Hey, listen man. The only thing you should be concerned about doing is helping out down at the Clinic. This girl is just a part of your dreams. Ok? Now, we're in reality that's what really matters ok? Remember that.

JEFF

Yea, you're right...Well, I need to get back to work. Let's see if I can get back through the doors.

BRAD

Givers, I tell you man, you're going to give so much there won't be anything left to give but your life? You ready for that responsibility?

Jeff's eyes travel back to the coffee shop and then back to the Mill.

Brad is ahead of him, making his way to the front of the line to gather as much food as the Keepers would allow him.

The Keepers were always in charge of the food, getting and giving.

Jeff is glad he is a Giver. He knows that he's making a difference in his World, not sure how much, but did it matter since they would all disappear into darkness after all?

CHAPTER ELEVEN

TRAPPED

Alisa sits alone out on the bleachers of an abandoned baseball field.

She looks out at the open space and then she feels Sage sit beside her.

SAGE

Your eyes, Alisa.

Alisa lets tears fall and Sage hold out his hands to catch them. He examines the teardrop and his demeanor changes.

ALISA

We will be no more. What have we done?

Alisa gets up and walks along the side of the baseball fence. Sage follows her but on the opposite side, peering at her through the metal wires that barely separate them.

ALISA

I feel so trapped. Trapped inside my own head. My own thoughts are hidden in my own head. And you are going to find them. You are going to rip them out of me. You are going to destroy me inside my own mind.

(pause)

We're turning against our own selves and I have to face my demons. Because that's what I'm going to have to silence before I will ever silence you.

Alisa gets to the opening of the baseball field and realizes that Sage is gone.

She sees a young girl and her father. He throws a ball and she hits it.

She runs as fast as she can until the father catches her and they laugh.

A ball rolls to Alisa's feet and she picks it up; but before she has a chance to throw the ball back to the two the field is empty once again.

In her hand now is a cellphone, ringing.
It's Sarah.

ALISA

It's Alisa.

SARAH

Alisa! Finally, I've been trying to get in touch with you all day.

ALISA

I...I don't know who this is.

SARAH

Hello! It's Sarah...you're sister...

ALISA

Sister...

SARAH

Alisa, are you doing ok?

ALISA

I'm fine. I just don't understand how...I don't have a sister.

SARAH

What? Are you sure you're feeling alright?

ALISA

I'm fine. I don't know why I would have created a sister...unless...I was so lonely…

A flashback plays in Alisa's head as she watches a Young Alisa in her room playing with dolls.

The house is quiet, other than the sweet laughter of a small child.

She has a cut out paper girl and it is sitting beside her.

ALISA

Sarah, what do you think about the name Raven? Do you think that's pretty?

(pause)

I will let you play with Annamarie, and Chloe.

(pause)

No! I always play with Sophie. Ok, maybe after I play with her, you can.

The sound of footsteps come up the stairs, and Dr. Fare walks up to hear Alisa talking to herself.

He pokes his head in and sees her playing by herself.

DR. FARE

Honey, who are you talking to?

ALISA

Oh, hi daddy, I'm just playing dolls with Sarah.

DR. FARE

Who's Sarah?

ALISA

She's my sister.

DR. FARE

Your sister, huh?

ALISA
Yea, she's really nice, and she always plays with me.

DR. FARE
Alisa, I'm sorry that you can't play with the other kids. Daddy knows how badly you want to and how important it is to your development, but daddy can't risk you getting exposed to the Virus. I'm sorry, sweetheart.

ALISA
It's ok daddy, I understand. I have Sarah.

DR. FARE
That's good, princess. I'm glad you made a new friend.

ALISA
She's not a friend daddy, she's my sister!

Dr. Fare looks at the cut out doll and it looks a little disturbing with it's dark black drawn holes for eyes and missing mouth.

He gets up and then leaves young Alisa alone to play.

Alisa comes back to her phone conversation but finds herself zoning in and out the conversation.

ALISA
Sarah, yes, sorry...I had a lapse in judgment...I'm sorry. You're the best sister in the world and thank you for calling to check up on me. I missed you...we'll have to meet up sometime and I'll have to see you, but—

A man crosses Alisa's field of vision and she recognizes him as Dr. Haggard.

He strolls into a building across the street.

ALISA

I really have to go, but I will definitely call you back later. Always thinking about you, love you, bye.

SARAH

Alisa, wait!

Alisa hangs up the phone and decides to follow him into the building.

CHAPTER TWELVE

INNER DEMONS

It's a therapist's office.
Alisa wanders inside, closely observing the pictures of mice on the walls, and the odd odor of exposed fears.

The receptionist carefully examines Alisa before getting her attention.

RECEPTIONIST

May I help you?

ALISA

Hi, uh, yes, I'm looking for a Dr. Haggard? Is he in?

RECEPTIONIST

He just got back from lunch, do you have an appointment with him?

ALISA

I'm not sure.

RECEPTIONIST

Let me check on that. What's your name?

ALISA

Alisa Fare.

RECEPTIONIST

Ah, yes, Ms. Fare. It's your first time with us. I just need you to fill out some paperwork and he'll be out to meet with you shortly.

Alisa goes to fill out the paperwork and then she waits, patiently.

Dr. Haggard finally comes out from the back.

DR. HAGGARD

Alisa?

Alisa gets up and she walks up to Dr. Haggard, who gives her a friendly smile.

DR. HAGGARD

Hello, Alisa, it's so nice to meet you. I'm Dr. Haggard, please follow me.

Alisa hesitates for moment, confused by his gentle demeanor. Alisa follows him to his room and she realizes it's a very warm, comfy place.

She sits down and notes a majestic view from his office.

A huge clear glass wall gives view of the whole city.

Dr. Haggard admires her awe. He also takes in her beauty as he scans over her pale brown skin, and noting her hazel eyes.

DR. HAGGARD

What a beautiful view, isn't it? How did I get so lucky.

(pause)

How can I help you today, Alisa?

ALISA

Dr. Haggard, we've met before.

DR. HAGGARD

We have? Well sure, it's a big city, I'm sure we may have come across each other and never have realized it.

ALISA

No, no. You were hunting me down...locking me up in the Ward. Trying to fix me...but nothing is broken.

DR. HAGGARD

I'm sorry Alisa...I don't recall.

He begins to write notes.

ALISA

No, of course not. Because I'm losing it. Tell me, Dr. Haggard. Can you fix me? Can you look into my demented world and make all the memories go away?

DR. HAGGARD

What memories, Alisa?

ALISA

I don't know, Doctor. I'm repressing memories and only you know how to get them to come out.

DR. HAGGARD

Tell me about your childhood.

ALISA

I had a great childhood. Dad did a great job of raising me on his own.

DR. HAGGARD

Single parent home, and I take it, an only child?

ALISA

Yes.

DR. HAGGARD

And why is that? What do you know about your mother?

ALISA

I don't have a mother.

DR. HAGGARD

Everyone has a mother. What did your father tell you about yours?

ALISA

I never asked.

DR. HAGGARD

All kids want to know.

ALISA

I didn't.

DR. HAGGARD

You felt rejected by your mother.

ALISA

I didn't have a mother. Daddy said I was a new creation.

DR. HAGGARD

Creation?

ALISA

I don't remember a lot of things.

DR. HAGGARD

You do remember, I can see the hurt in your eyes.

ALISA

(remembering)

I couldn't do anything. I had to stay in the house.

DR. HAGGARD

Why Alisa? Why couldn't you play with all the other little kids?

ALISA

Daddy said I had to stay healthy.

DR. HAGGARD

Why, Alisa?

ALISA

He wouldn't tell me.

DR. HAGGARD

He wanted to keep you safe? From what, Alisa? What did he want to keep you safe from?

ALISA

Sage.

Dr. HAGGARD

Sage?

ALISA

From Sage...Sage attacked his brain...it turned him against himself...it destroyed our family.

DR. HAGGARD

But what about you, little Alisa? What happened to you?

ALISA

I went away.

DR. HAGGARD

Where did they take you?

ALISA

(tearing up)

No, I don't want to go there.

DR. HAGGARD

They closed you off to society Alisa. They trapped you in a tiny room and watched you, day in and day out, like they are doing right now. Watching your every move. This is the first time in your life when you don't have to listen to anyone else, or have to do what they say. You can embrace Sage. You can stay here forever and be free. I know that's what you really want, Alisa. They are just using you anyway. Do you really want to go back and help them? They created your life, and now this is finally your chance to redeem yourself.

Dr. Haggard rises up and walks toward the window to overlook the city.

DR. HAGGARD

You want to see your repressed memories? Here you go.

The room darkens, and Alisa watches herself inside the large glass window.

She stands in a white room wearing all white.
The room is bare except for a little mirror and a small cot that they provide for her.

A video camera keeps her under constant surveillance mounted in the top corner of her room.

She is sedated and sleeping on a small, uncomfortable cot.
A few nurses come in and out the room giving her routine injections and monitor her eating.

They watch everything she does. She's trapped, alone and isolated from society.

She interacts only with Robin.
Robin opens a small screen in the center of the door to peer inside to see Alisa.

ROBIN

Hey, how are you feeling today?

ALISA

(angry)
Robin, how much longer are you going to keep me here?

ROBIN
Whoa, take it easy Ally, we had to do this. You agreed to all of this.

ALISA
Why? Why did you force me to do this?

ROBIN
(repeating)
We didn't force you, you volunteered.

ALISA
No. I'm not even a person! My father took away all my rights. I'm just a clone. Created to be a cure! I've had no choice in this, you predetermined my life.

ROBIN
You're going to save humanity.

ALISA
(furious)
I wasn't given a choice. No free will. I don't want to do this anymore. Let me out!

ROBIN
Alisa, you're being selfish.

ALISA
Selfish!

ROBIN
(quietly)
We didn't think you could be.

ALISA

What did you think I could be?

ROBIN

It won't be too much longer now...

ALISA

I just want my own life!

ROBIN

There is no life outside of these walls, Alisa. We're all Sick. You are our last hope, and if you want to think about yourself right now, then fine. But we're trying to save humanity, with or without your consent Nobody has free will anymore.

Robin shuts the small sliding door leaving Alisa alone to cry and think about her fate.

Alisa is now standing by the glass window with her hand extended, reaching toward her reflection in the window.
She looks back to Dr. Haggard and shutters.

DR. HAGGARD

I think we should meet regularly until we make you better.

ALISA
(defeated)

Ok.

Alisa inches out the room and Dr. Haggard watches her go. She leaves the office in a shocked state, then runs into Jeff again as he comes for his appointment.

JEFF

Alisa!

ALISA

Jeff!

JEFF

We keep bumping into each other. So you're seeing Dr. Haggard as well?

ALISA

Yes.

JEFF

Is everything ok?

ALISA

Yea, I'm fine.

JEFF

Well, it's so good to see you again.

ALISA

(blurts)

I need you.

JEFF

What?

ALISA

I need to feel you.

Alisa finds herself pulling Jeff close to her.
She embraces him and they stay there for what seems like eternity.

JEFF

Alisa? What's going on?

ALISA

You're real!

JEFF

Hey, you know, I don't really need to see this guy this week. I think that was the best therapy I've gotten in a while. Wanna get out of here?

ALISA

Please.

Alisa and Jeff both leave. Dr. Haggard walks out to the waiting room to call Jeff's name.
He frowns and gives the receptionist a cold look.

CHAPTER THIRTEEN

LOVE

They enter Jeff's living room and Alisa realizes that everything is very familiar.

She looks back at the oblong picture of a clock.

JEFF

Would you like some coffee? Tea?

ALISA

Oh, you don't have to worry about making it, let me.

Alisa walks into the other room, which turns into the kitchen. Jeff watches her in shock as she moves around his kitchen with ease.

ALISA

I know my way around a kitchen, what can I say.

JEFF

You're a keeper then!

They both laugh and then they sit down and talk.

JEFF

So, the last time I saw you...I swear I thought you were telling me about a lady named Robin....and this thing about Sage...

ALISA

Yes, I did. You remembered...did you tell her?

JEFF

Alisa...I...I don't know what that has to do with anything.

ALISA

You know about the Virus though, don't you?

JEFF

Yea, I do...but why is that so important to you?

ALISA

Jeff, I don't want you to run away again.

JEFF

I'm just trying to understand.

ALISA

No, we don't have to talk about it right now.

JEFF

Ok, I'm just trying to help.

ALISA

You're not lucid yet.

JEFF

Lucid?

ALISA

It's when you can control your dreams. They used to talk about it in the lab all the time. That's the only way I'll be able to communicate with you effectively.

JEFF

Who are "they"?

ALISA

The scientists.

JEFF

Okay...

ALISA

I haven't seen Sage in a while.

JEFF

Sage? The Virus?

ALISA

In this world, or should I say in my world, I've personified him as a human named Sage, and I don't know why.

JEFF

Ok, so this Sage guy...tell me about him?

ALISA

It's the Virus inside my mind, trying to destroy my brain. It's what's making us all Sick, out in the real world.

Jeff stares at Alisa as she says this, then nearly spits out his coffee.

He laughs nervously.

Absurd-

JEFF

You actually believe this?

ALISA

This is the truth. It lives in each of us that has been exposed to the Virus. I'm just trying to figure out a way I can eliminate the Virus out of my system before any irreparable damage is done to my brain.

JEFF

You're serious?

ALISA

I don't see what's funny. This Virus is killing millions, and you know this. You have to wake up to the nightmare every day and hope that it's all a bad dream, but it's not. I'm sure by now you're hoping that this is your waking life and that's the dream world you go back to.

JEFF

I know what Sage is, and what the effects are. I'm a Giver. I take care of the patients. But there's no way that this Sage person is real, and is a walking Virus out to take over your brain. That's absurd.

ALISA

Jeff, I hope you can understand one day. I hope you can take control of your brain and become lucid, and I pray that it's not too late for you.

Suddenly Jeff freezes before her eyes.
She waves her hand in front of him but he doesn't respond.
A flash of light catches her attention in her peripheral vision, locking her into a trance.
She follows the flashing light into the bathroom and peers into the mirror to see Robin, Ethan, and herself.

They are in the lab overlooking Alisa's body and checking her vital stats right after the injection.

ETHAN

She's hit the hour mark. Stats still seem normal. Are you just going to stand there the whole time? You're going to have to get rest or eat at some point.

ROBIN

I'm fine.

ETHAN

You haven't taken you're eyes off of her.

ROBIN

I said I'm fine. I'm just being extra cautious. I want to be here if she wakes up.

ETHAN

I have a feeling that it's going to be at least a couple days or more before she wakes up.

ROBIN

I'm sorry Alisa. I'm sorry for what I said.

Ethan lowers his head and allows them to be alone.

ROBIN

I didn't mean any of those words, you have a will. And after all of this is over, you will get to choose your own destiny. I'll make sure of it. You will get to save the world; this is what's best for you. I only did this because we loved you. I hope one day you can understand that.

Alisa tries to reach out to Robin but instead she is slowly sucked back out, back into Reverie.

CHAPTER FOURTEEN

SAGE, COME BACK

The darkness evaporates as fast as the light appears.
Alisa has an impression of arms wrapping around her as she becomes conscious again.

It's only Jeff.
She breathes a sigh of relief but it's short-lived.

JEFF

What? Were you expecting Sage?

ALISA

No, should I be?

JEFF

No, but you talk about him all the time.

ALISA

Because he's real, Jeff...

(under her breath)

You never listen to me.

JEFF

Here we go again.

How could she get him to understand?
The World of Reevie keeps her on her toes, she couldn't expect anything.

Nothing in Reevie made any sense, since dreams sometimes have their hidden meanings.

One conversation leads to another at a different time, somewhere lost in space.

All the memories she had experienced with Jeff were created by her subconscious mind.

Or were they?

Jeff is in love with her;

She feels it.

And yet, it's Sage she desires; deep down,

It's Sage she needs.

After a lingering moment, Alisa follows a light banging sound coming from outside the bathroom into the darkened living room.

Gasping,

Sage stands near an open window, panting heavily.

SAGE

Alisa.

ALISA

Where have you been?!

Jeff pursues Alisa to the living room but he doesn't see Sage.

JEFF

I've been helping patients all day…and it's just confusing when you talk to me about things that are…

ALISA

(interrupting)

No, not you.

JEFF

What are you talking about?

ALISA

You don't see him?

JEFF

Who?

ALISA

Sage! He's right there...

JEFF

Alisa...I...I don't know what to do with you anymore. It's always Sage with you, you're always seeing him, chasing after him...he's ruining our lives.

ALISA

But, he's right there.

JEFF

No one's there.

ALISA

I can't be here right now. Sage, what are you doing here, where have you been?

SAGE

(emotionless)

You left me.

ALISA

No I didn't, I couldn't...you left me at the baseball field...

SAGE

You love Jeff.

ALISA

No, I barely know him.

JEFF

Alisa? I'm calling your sister. You need to talk to someone.

ALISA

Jeff, what are you doing? You can't see him, he's right here. Sage talk to him!

Jeff pulls out his phone to begins to make the call.

JEFF

Hey Sarah, I'm sorry if this is a bad time, but I need you to talk to your sister. She's losing it.

ALISA

Why does he feel that he knows me? We've only been out a few times.

JEFF

Alisa, how can you say that—I love you.

ALISA

Sage...what's going on?

Finally, everything is silent and Sage walks up to Alisa. He holds out his hand and Alisa takes it.

Blackout-

CHAPTER FIFTEEN

REAL LOVE?

Alisa and Sage are walking amongst many shops and they see Alisa and Jeff enter many places together.

They get ice cream,
Visit the park,
Ice skate,
Go for a walk,
And stare into each other eyes.
They visit Central Park and make a wish in the fountain.

ALISA

No, those aren't real. Those aren't real memories, Sage.

SAGE

They were real to you.

ALISA

No. You put them there. That isn't fair.

SAGE

Are you sure? Take a look again.

Alisa becomes aware of the moment as she looks into Jeff's eyes right before they kiss.

Alisa pulls away, and Jeff frowns.

JEFF

Something I said?

ALISA

No. I...I don't remember why we're here.

JEFF

Well, I was just telling you, how special you are...and how much I love spending all this time with you lately. You've been so great. I'm really glad I met you.

ALISA

Jeff, this can't be really happening. I haven't met you in real life...and you've fallen in love with me?

JEFF

I'm sorry. But I have.

ALISA

It's not possible. I barely know you.

JEFF

And that's what is so great about us. We don't have to know everything…we just feel it. I can't explain it, but I just know it.

ALISA

Jeff...I feel it too, but I can't explain it.

JEFF

You don't have to explain love; just let it happen.

ALISA

(searching Jeff's eyes)

You really feel it?

JEFF

I do. I can't stop thinking about you. I love you.

Alisa kisses Jeff passionately, then she pulls back to look at him.

ALISA

I'm sorry Jeff, this moment isn't real.

Alisa races off, back into the darkness Sage has caused within her.

CHAPTER SIXTEEN

ROOFTOPS

Rooftops
Provide a sense of comfort.
A sense of openness, and oneness with the World.
Sometimes, it makes people come alive.
At times it makes them cower back into the ruins of their sad lives.
For Alisa,
Rooftops makes her want to dance.
She dangles her legs over the edge, ready to jump at any moment.
The sound of a couple of footsteps grab her attention.
He's come back for her.

ALISA

You didn't stop me.

SAGE

What did you find?

ALISA

You can't kill yourself in a dream and die in reality.

(pause)

I didn't even wake up, I just found myself back here.

(realizes)

This is Hell.

SAGE

Did it hurt?

ALISA

There is no physical pain here.

SAGE

(curious)

Were you afraid?

ALISA

No. I was fearless. My thoughts were blank.

Alisa closes her eyes and pictures it again.
Falling, over and over.
Sage watches her face morph into exhaustion as she looks down into an endless pit below her.

ALISA (V.O)

I wanted to be as close to death as I possibly could. Because they told me that after death comes peace.

Alisa watches herself falling,
She looks back up, only to see Sage's sickened face glaring at her.

ALISA

I'm a science experiment. Do I even have a soul? What happens to me after death? Where do I go? Here?

SAGE

(reassuring)

You have a soul. Jeff connected with your soul.

ALISA

Maybe so. But I was never given a choice. I'm going to be reborn. And maybe this time, death can take me.

Alisa lets go of the edge and begins her plummet into the pit of her inner demons that reach up to pull her further and further down into nothingness.

CHAPTER SEVENTEEN

LUCID

Dr. Haggard's office remains isolated and is deteriorating. Jeff's anxiety has gotten the best of him as he pushes his way through the crusting doors in search of answers and healing.

Dr. Haggard is staring out his window, out to the unknown World that is beginning to fall apart.

DR. HAGGARD
Ah, what a nice surprise to see you, Jeff. How are you feeling today?

JEFF
I'm fine. I'm just worried about my girlfriend.

DR. HAGGARD
Ah, you're still seeing Ms. Fare?

JEFF
Yea. Lately, she's gotten worse. She keeps talking about this Sage guy. And now she's starting to see him everywhere. I just don't know what to do anymore. I feel like I'm going crazy.

DR. HAGGARD
Those are very normal reactions for a loved one. I haven't seen Alisa in a while. But, maybe it's time to pay her a visit.

JEFF
I would really appreciate it. I need all the help I can get.

DR. HAGGARD
Don't worry, we'll get her better in no time.
(pause)

Oh, and Jeff, you really should think about trying to get yourself better. Wouldn't want to see you here in the Ward, would we?

Jeff shudders at the thought of himself strapped to a bed, just as Alisa was.

Silence, sometimes, is the best response.

DR. HAGGARD

You don't look very well these days. Something else on your mind that you want to tell me about?

A flash strikes the ceiling,
Trickling into Jeff's dilated pupils.

DR. HAGGARD

You don't want to go down her path, boy. It's a dangerous road—and no one comes back the same.

There is a brief pause until a shrieking sound sends Jeff into a ball on the ground cradling his face.

JEFF

What's happening to me?

A seething Screecher rushes into the room with its fangs protruding.

Saliva oozes out of its mouth onto the floor near Jeff's face. It locks eye contact with Jeff cautiously examining his next moves.

JEFF

(fading)

Stay away from Alisa.

Jeff swiftly grabs a nearby chair and pushes it over onto the Screecher as he makes his escape to the exit.

However, the Screecher is too quick— it grabs Jeff by his shirt and hurls him into the glass window, shattering it, and Jeff falls into Reality.

Jeff awakens at the Lab as other frantically pass by him. A clipboard is in his hand with a few patient names on the paper.

His eyes scan the page to see where he left off, but a nurse passes by, knocking the sheet out of his hands.

A few people are clawing at each other and fighting in the hallways as some nurses try to calm the situation.

A familiar nurse with mousey brown hair rushes up to Jeff in a panic.

Blood is spattered on her uniform.

NURSE

We're running out of supplies.

JEFF

Check the overflow cabinet.

NURSE

We've already been through all the cabinets. We have nothing left. We're going to have to close the doors.

JEFF

We can't close the clinic down.

NURSE

There's nothing more we can do for these people. We're all entering Phase 4. There is no more hope.

There is complete chaos all around them, all hope has been forgotten.

A few of the patients are coughing up blood near Jeff. Finally, he makes his way outside the clinic to catch his breath.

His heartbeats thud in his ears and the air around him throws him off balance.

He holds onto the building as he allows his nose to bleed, signaling to him that he is now in Phase 3.

Dr. Thompkins, an older gentleman with an oversized white coat calmly approaches Jeff.

DR. THOMPKINS

Well, I think it's about that time we shut it down, young man.

JEFF

We can't just turn these people away that need our help. Where else are they going to go?

DR. THOMPKINS

To prepare for their deaths.

JEFF

You can't be serious. You're a doctor, you save lives.

DR. THOMPKINS

You don't look so good yourself. What phase are you in, Jeff?

JEFF

It doesn't matter.

DR. THOMPKINS

We don't want to put any more people in danger. You're in Phase 3 aren't you?

JEFF

I'm fine.

DR. THOMPKINS

Go home, boy. Spend as much time with your family as possible, while you still can.

JEFF

You're going to shut the doors. I won't let you do that.

DR. THOMPKINS

We have no other choice. No one is well, and I can't think clearly. We need someone who can run things with a clear mind. Go home, Jeff. I'm sorry it has to be this way.

Jeff realizes that he is starting to waver in and out. He picks himself off the wall.

JEFF

(revealing)

You're the closest to family I've ever had. Where else can I go? I don't have anyone else.

DR. THOMPKINS

I won't let you die in a clinic. You deserve better than that. You deserve better than me. I promised your father.

Dr. Thompkins helps Jeff to his feet, guiding him away from the clinic.

JEFF

What's going to happen to you?

DR. THOMPKINS

I'm going to join you, We've lost the fight…it's over. We can go home.

JEFF

You promise?

DR. THOMPKINS

I promise.

They look at each intensely before Jeff falls onto the Doctor's own unsteady body.

Dr. Thompkins shows his age as he lifts Jeff up with his shaky arms.

DR. THOMPKINS

Now, please…stay on the path, go straight home with the others. Get out of the city.

Jeff peers into Dr. Thompkins' warm gray eyes.
He nods, then leaves without another word.

The path is endless as it continues to stretches on and on. Jeff holds onto his side as he limps along, passing by a few patients with bright red eyes and bleeding noses.

A young girl wearing a nurse's gown backtracks through the crowd when she sees Jeff take a dive to the earth's hard ground.

Her smile triggers a memory of a girl he thinks he remembers from a dream.

This girl is an old friend, sweet Keely.

KEELY

Jeff, are you ok?

JEFF

I'm fine. I just need a moment.

KEELY

Yes, of course, do you need any water?

JEFF

No, I'm fine.

He falls once more onto her, coughing up more blood as it drips out of his mouth onto her skin.

KEELY

Here, let me help you, let's sit for a minute.

JEFF

(out of breath)

I need water.

KEELY

Yes. Yes, of course, here you go.

Keely takes off her backpack and searches through its contents to find a canteen filled with water.

She slowly pours it into his mouth and he gulps it down. A few books fall out of Keely's backpack and catch Jeff's eye.

One particular book catches his attention as he reads the cover: LUCID DREAMING.

JEFF

Lucid dreaming...that's an interesting concept. Why are you reading that?

KEELY

Yea, it's fascinating, I'm actually almost done reading it. It's a pretty cool concept. I've only attempted it a few times...only could stay aware part of the time. I've heard it can be a wild experience if you can stay lucid for the whole dream.

(pause)

It provides an escape out of this Virtual Reality we're all stuck in sometimes…this way, I can understand what's going on inside me.

JEFF

(quickly)

So it is possible? We can go there? We can control our dreams? What does it say you have to do?

KEELY

Hold on, settle down! I mean...I'm basically done with the book if you want to see for yourself.

JEFF

Thank you.

Jeff takes the book and eagerly scans the pages.
Although he tries to focus on the words in front of him, all he can think about is the girl that helps him find freedom in his dreams, and Sage, the one whom she keeps reminding him, it's only just that, a dream.

KEELY

Yea, maybe you will have better luck with it than me. Or maybe, in the time we live in, it's not so hard after all. We are a pill nation, aren't we?

She holds up a red pill in her hand, and it calls out to him.
All it took is a simple pill?
Where had their society gone?
They are lost,
Searching for anything to fill the void.
Wishing and hoping that in some way they can find connection, but they strayed far away,
Seeking to fill the space by turning inward.
The city crumbles, screaming for the way it used to be.
When people were happy with Mother Nature, and when the digital world didn't swallow them up.
Now, the disease is swallowing them up, the Virus of the mind.
And no one is immune, not yet.
One was rising,
The girl without a choice.

Jeff has a choice, and he consumes it.
Down goes the little red bullet,

Down the tantalizing rabbit hole.

CHAPTER EIGHTEEN

LUCID

KEELY
I need you to lay back and pay attention to your breathing.

Jeff lays on a pallet he's made out of his sweatshirt and a few blankets Keely had stuffed into her bag.
Concentrating, he slows his breath to a constant pace.

KEELY
First, set your alarm on your wristwatch at about 2 hours to make sure you know you have induced REM.

The alarm button on his watch chimes as it sets in place at 2 hours.

KEELY
Try meditating for the first 20 minutes until sleep sets in. Repeat, "Am I dreaming?". Stay completely relaxed and still. Become aware of your surroundings. Focus.
(pause)
What are you trying to accomplish?

JEFF
I need to find Alisa.

KEELY
Alisa? Uhm. Ok, focus on her face. The details of her eyes, her smile, her smell, anything you can remember.

(she scans the book beside her)

You can try the FILD method; move your index finger up and down and with your other hand pinch your nose. Keep repeating that, think of it as if you are counting sheep.

JEFF

No, that's stupid, I can't do that.

KEELY

Ok, what about trying to mark your hand with an A for "Awake"? Is that any better?

JEFF

No, it's better…My mind keeps slipping.

Keely thinks for a beat, until her eyes light up.

KEELY

I know! This has to do the trick.

She turns on a recording of binaural beats on a small recorder she retrieves from her jacket pocket.

KEELY

Now repeat, "I am dreaming."

JEFF

I am dreaming…I am dreaming…I am dreaming…

(feeling more relaxed)

Alright, Alisa...You want me to get lucid, here I come.

He continues to repeat "I am dreaming," and her face pops up.

Gentle, elegant, sweet Alisa.

Her brown hair flows onto his skin as he feels its silky smoothness, pressing it between his fingers.

Her cheeks blush a warm red tone as she pulls away, teasing him to chase after her, to want her, and he does.

Alisa runs through a wooded area until she gets to a deep pond.

The beauty of the pond mesmerizes her as she stands near the edge peering into the depth of the still waters.

A bridge made of timber spreads across the center with bright maroon railings.

Alisa steps onto the wooden planks, looking back over her shoulder, hoping to see him.

Him, Jeff hopes, is himself,
But Sage is never too far away.

JEFF

Alisa! Alisa!

ALISA

Jeff? Jeff!

(out of breath)

Jeff, there's not much time left.

Confused, yet grateful to be near her, he melts in her sight.

JEFF

You came back!

ALISA

Yes, I came back...

JEFF

I was waiting for you. I'm always here waiting for you. I know you will come back.

ALISA

Jeff, please listen to me. I love you. Have you figured out how to get lucid? If not, I will help you.

JEFF

Lucid.

ALISA

Yes, lucid. I told you that the only way to make sense of all this is to become lucid. Are you aware?

JEFF

I don't know what you are talking about.

ALISA

No, no, no. Don't you leave me now! Don't you wake up! I need you.

JEFF

I don't understand.

ALISA

Jeff, none of this is real, you are in a dream. Everything here would be absurd and be too wild to be reality. Does this happen in reality? I don't have a reflection!

Alisa stands on the bridge above the water but no reflection is present on the water.
Jeff looks back at her and slowly comes to lucidity.
He pinches his nose, but he can still breathe.

JEFF

Am I dreaming? This is a dream. I'm inside my dream.

Finally, his pupils begin to dilate, bringing him into consciousness.

JEFF

My God. Are you...are you lucid as well? Or am I creating you?

ALISA

Thank God, Jeff...Listen to me carefully. I am real. I am lucid.

I've been sedated and put, unconscious, in a testing facility a few miles away from the city at Fare Corps. It's a lab where they have been doing research for the past 20 years on the S.A.G.E virus.

JEFF

Yes, the S.A.G.E Virus that's been attacking our world. I'm aware of the research being done there. So it is true! They are still working on a cure.

ALISA

Yes. I can't go much into detail because we don't have much time, but I need you to bring a message to my team—Robin Leighman. Tell her that I'm doing my best. That Sage is more powerful than I expected and I don't know if we can kill the Virus. There has to be another way, but reassure her, I'm doing everything I can to stop Sage....and tell her...she has nothing to be sorry about. She made the right decision.

JEFF

That's a lot to unload on someone.

ALISA

Jeff, I know this all seems crazy right now, but you have to trust me. You will find me if you go there, get to Fare Corps. You'll see.

JEFF

This is impossible, improbable. How is this even possible?

ALISA

It just is. There are pathways for our souls to interact with each other. I'll never understand it, and I don't think we're meant to. It just means we have so much more to discover about ourselves.

JEFF

What is this place?

ALISA

It's the place when you…

JEFF

When I first told you I loved you.

ALISA

Yes. You remember?

JEFF

How could I ever forget? It was real wasn't it?

ALISA

(unsure)

I don’t know.

JEFF

I will give them your message. But what about you, now? What does this mean?

ALISA

It means that my mind is going to start shutting down soon and I won't know real memories from false ones. My mind will be my worst enemy. The Virus will either consume me, or I'll find another way.

Alisa and Jeff lock eyes a powerful stance.
Alisa is unsure of what to do, but Jeff is.
He wants to embrace her,
She holds her ground as the tension around them builds.
Words begin to rise up within her,
UNTIL…all of a sudden, Jeff disappears.

A loud chime awakens Jeff as he lays on Keely's cold blankets. He quickly searches for a piece of paper to write down the message he was given in the dream.

He tears off the paper and picks himself off the ground.

KEELY

Is everything ok? Where are you going?

JEFF

Is there any way I can access a car?

A cold stare,
Leaves Jeff waiting.

But he knows Keely always has something up her sleeves; or, if not up her sleeves, in that bag of hers.

And that's where she goes,
She pulls out a small set of silver keys.

A small golden hawk hangs off the keychain.

Jeff nods his head and gives Keely a small kiss on her forehead.

JEFF

(whispers)

Thank you.

His mind resets its focus on the outskirts of the city, going directly to Fare Corps.

One day he would be able to go home again, but it is only to settle and die.

He isn't ready to die just yet.
There is life out there, and he wants to make sure he finds it.

Fare Corps is the key; the only problem is getting past the bolted doors.

There is a small voice inside telling him to keep going, and he knows, deep down,

It's Alisa.
Trapped in another time,
and yet, still so close to his heart.

CHAPTER NINETEEN

TEMPERATURE

The temperature in Reevie is increasing, and Alisa is alone in the dark and dreary world.

She finds herself peeling off her jacket,
Sage watches her from the shadows.

ALISA

What's happening to me?

SAGE

What's wrong with Alisa?

ALISA

I'm burning up.

Sage points to the water in the pond near them,
She nods her head as she lowers her feet into the chilly liquid.

With an expeditious stride she hops into the water but then realizes it's just as hot as she is.

She swims back to the edge as Sage watches her.

SAGE

Better?

ALISA

No.

Sage bends down to touch the water and all of a sudden it turns ice cold. Alisa tries to climb out of it.

ALISA

What are you doing! Stop it!

The fight begins to take over her body as she slips further into the now murky waters.

Sage stares at her,
Enamored, yet oblivious of how he can help her,

Back in the lab, Robin notices the spike in Alisa's temperature on the monitor.

She watches it rise and then she calls in some of the lab assistants.

ROBIN

We need ice packs immediately, come on, come on! Alisa, you've got to fight it off.

The scientists bring in the ice packs and pull Alisa out of the tank and try to cool off her body.

She is burning up.

LACEY

Phase 2 has begun.

Alisa pulls herself out of the frigid waters by digging her nails into the grass near the edge of the pond.

She uses all the energy she has left to pull herself out.

Once out of the pond she storms pass Sage, going in the direction of her home to cool herself off.

She enters her house and goes straight to her bedroom.
A compact window catches her eyes and she throws it open to feel a mild breeze.

It helps, but her skin is still warm to the touch.
She takes a look around the room, then notices a notebook on the nightstand.

It's the book she grabbed earlier when she fled the house, when Dr. Haggard attacked her.

She flips open the pages and sees that it's her old journal she kept as a child.

She reads it out loud to herself.

ALISA

Dear Dairy, ugh, that sounds cheesy, no one says dear dairy anymore. Hello world. My name is Alisa Fare. I come from a long line of Fare relatives, all of importance. I have a perfect family, which consists of a father, a mother, and my younger sister Sarah. My life is amazing. I can do what I want and stay out as late as I want. All my friends are pretty cool. They come over all the time. And well, of course I know you're dying to know who I'm dating. His name is Chet. He's a soccer player. One of the best. He calls me Princess. Our first kiss was under a moonlit star on a bridge. He told me he loved me. I hope dad approves. Love is a wonderful thing. I hope everyone gets to experience it, because life would suck if we didn't.

Alisa skims over more pages and out pops a picture of her and her father.

She grabs the photo and places it beside her on the nightstand but it falls down.

There is writing on the back.

Dr. Fare's voice booms through the room, playing in her head.

DR. FARE

Alisa, I love you with every inch of my being. I'm sorry it has to be this way. And baby, if this Virus gets to me before my work is complete, please know that this wasn't just a science experiment. You became so much more to me....

Alisa looks up to see that her father has entered her room and is talking to her.

ALISA

(weakly)

Daddy?

DR. FARE

Alisa, I never got to apologize to you.

ALISA

Dad, you don't have to apologize.

DR. FARE

Yes, I do.

ALISA

You wanted to help the world.

DR. FARE

I thought that's what I was doing—until I realized that you are the world. And I wasn't helping you. I was hurting you. I kept you away from everything that mattered. Everything you dreamed about.

ALISA

To protect me. I know that now.

DR. FARE

I wanted you to have a good life! I wanted you to be healthy. I was a father, and you grew on me. I didn't want them to touch you, poke and prod you. I wanted you to be free to make your own decisions.

ALISA

Dad, I'm glad Robin kept your research going. If it wasn't for her...we'd all be doomed. I want to live, Daddy. For us.

They embrace.

DR. FARE

This life, after all this madness, isn't so bad. I'd have given anything just to see your face again in my old life. Now I get to see you whenever I like.

ALISA

I was never too far from your heart.

DR. FARE

Love is the only thing that we have that lasts. That's what we should cling to, and hope for.

ALISA

Love might be the cure.

(pause)

I've missed you daddy. It's so good to see you again!

Robin is still fixated on the stats, but Alisa's temperature has dropped a lot.

However, they hit another problem when they notice how cold she is becoming.

ROBIN

What's going on now?

LACEY

Her stats are going the reverse now. We need to get this ice off of her ASAP.

ROBIN

Ok. Come on.

They begin to remove the ice packs.

In Alisa's Reverie, she looks outside the window and notices that it's snowing.

She lights the gas fireplace in the living room and wraps a fluffy blanket around herself.

A steam of her frosty breath appears in front of her as she paces around the house wondering where Sage is.

ALISA

Is this how it's going to end?

Sage saunters into the room, his eyes focus on Alisa. She holds her hands near the fire, trying to stay warm. Her face is pale and sickly.

SAGE

(repeating)

What's wrong with Alisa?

ALISA

(snapping)

Sage, you can't keep asking me what's wrong. I don't think there is anything you can do to help me.

SAGE

I want to help you.

ALISA

You've helped me enough.

SAGE

You're getting sick.

ALISA

Yes, Sage, I'm dying.

SAGE

No.

ALISA

Yes. You're a Virus, Sage, you're the Virus in my body attacking my mind. Ever since I've been in this world I can't stop seeing things I don't want to see. It's nonstop. No breaks. No rest periods. It feels like eternity.

(realizing)
There is no end.

SAGE
I don't want to hurt you, Alisa.

ALISA
Why did you say that?

He stares at her,
And her heart skips a beat.
She knows what he's about to say,
And she doesn't want him to say it.

SAGE
I love you.

ALISA
You....love me? You can't love me.

SAGE
I do.

ALISA
Why do you love me?

SAGE
Someone has to be on your side.

ALISA
What?

SAGE
You don't want to hurt me.

ALISA

No, I don't want to hurt you.

SAGE

Sage will not let Alisa die.

ALISA

It's not about dying Sage, help me to not lose my mind.

Suddenly a loud bang is heard outside the house and a rock is hurled through the windows.

Sage quickly grabs Alisa and hurries her along to a safe place to take cover.

SAGE

Wait here.

ALISA

Sage, no!

Sage pushes Alisa into a closet,
She bangs on the door trying to free herself, but Sage locks it by sealing the door with his scorching claws.

ALISA

Sage! Let me out!

She stops after she hears a loud bang coming from the other side.

Dr. Haggard bursts into the room along with a few Screechers.
He demands Alisa to come.

She holds her breath so he won't hear her.
He stops in front of the closet door and just as he's about to alert a Screecher,

Sage appears behind him.

SAGE

Leave Alisa alone.

DR. HAGGARD

(laughing)

You've got to be kidding me.

(pause)

Sage, huh? Well, this is new. You're protecting her now, instead of trying to destroy her?

SAGE

I love her.

DR. HAGGARD

You love her? Pathetic. You can't love her. You don't belong here, remember. She's trying to get rid of you. You're a Virus, Sage. Your only mission is to kill your host.

SAGE

No.

DR. HAGGARD

You're very confused, I see. You asked for my help. You brought her to me. Remember that, Sage? I wouldn't be here if it wasn't for you.

SAGE

Stop it.

DR. HAGGARD

Don't turn your back now. Finish the job.

SAGE

No!

Sage lunges at Dr. Haggard but a Screecher intervenes.

They tackle each other on the ground while Dr. Haggard goes through the house searching for Alisa.

Sage grabs the beast and throws it around the room. It screeches and attacks Sage, driving him into a wall. Sage's arm darkens and he is able to get close enough to stab his arm through the fiend, as it cries out in pain.

CHAPTER TWENTY

AWAKENS

The silence in the lab is excruciating, except for the Pod room.
Alisa thrashes around violently.
They quickly extract her from the Pod and with all their strength they try to restrain her.
Sadly,
There is nothing anybody can do.

ETHAN
We can't give her anymore sedative... she's just going to have to get past this attack.

ROBIN
I haven't seen the Virus take over as quickly as it has with her. She'll be in Phase 3 within seconds.

ETHAN
Robin, all we can do is wait.

LACEY
Come quick, you have to see this!

They follow her out to the hallway overlooking the front of the building and see that there are hundreds of people gathering outside Fare Corp,s trying to break down the doors to get inside.

ROBIN
My God. Are we safe? Is there any way they can get in?

ETHAN

There's always a way to get in... enough pressure could blow the doors wide open.

LACEY

Even if we found a cure, how would we be able to help all these people? We barely have any Phase 1's left.

ROBIN

Ethan, lock up the right wing. We can't let them get to her.

Ethan and Lacey look at each other, then Ethan goes to secure the area while Lacey stays.

LACEY

What's your grand plan now Robin? What are those things?

ROBIN

I don't care what you overheard, or what's going on in that head of yours, but right now, we're a team and our hope rests on that girl in that tank. I suggest if you're going to be a hindrance, you should go out and be with the rest of them.

Lacey's nose begins to bleed and she sways a little.

ROBIN

Which it looks like you'll be, soon enough, Phase 5, An Ailing.

Robin holds her ground as Lacey rips through her.

LACEY

(horrified)

You don't have a plan. This is it.

ROBIN

No I don't. She's going to pull through. That is my plan.

Below, amongst the raging crowd, we that see Jeff is on foot. He charges through the aggressive citizens until he reaches the entrance.

JEFF
(shouting)
Alisa! ALISA! Robin Leighman!

The surveillance camera locks on Jeff and captures a photo of him up close.
He pounds on the door with amazing force.
His pain is intense, real, and Jeff feels true agony and urgency.
Robin is in an intense standoff with Lacey until another scientist interrupts them.

SCIENTIST
Robin, we have an urgent message for you. We have someone who would like to speak with you on the matter of Alisa.

ROBIN
(shocked)
Yes?

SCIENTIST
We have a gentleman here, by the name of Jeffrey Neal, who has been in contact with Alisa via dreams and visions. He would like to speak with you. He has a message he would like to relay to you from her.

ROBIN
(suspicious)
Bring him in.

Robin is waiting in the conference room. Jeff is brought in. She eyes him carefully, noting his dirty jeans and bloody t-shirt.
His boyish face relaxes her, prompting her to stand up and shake his hand.

ROBIN

Jeffrey Neal? It's nice to meet you, I'm Robin Leighman.

JEFF

You can call me Jeff, Finally a face to a name.

ROBIN

(small smile)

So, my understanding is that you've come here today to tell me something about Alisa?

JEFF

I know Alisa very well, Robin. She's told me everything.

ROBIN

Has she now?

JEFF

You keep her locked up in some vault of water and allow this Virus to run through her mind.

ROBIN

(shocked)

How could you possibly know this?

JEFF

She comes to me, in my dreams. Detailed visions and dreams.

ROBIN

It's not possible. You've never met her in person before.

JEFF

I haven't; and I can't explain it either, but I know her.

ROBIN

What has she told you?

JEFF

She wanted me to give you a message.

(pause)

She said that she's doing her best and Sage is more powerful than she expected. She doesn't know how she can kill the Virus but she's trying everything she can.

ROBIN

Thank you.

JEFF

She also told me you have nothing to be sorry about, and you made the right decision.

ROBIN

How did you manage to connect with her as you did?

JEFF

It's called lucid dreaming. I can help you get to her.

Robin watches him carefully, but then she nods.

CHAPTER TWENTY-ONE

THE CLOSET

All is silent.,
Alisa peeks through the lock.
The fighting has stopped, and she is alone.
There is a faint screeching sound, so she pulls her head back toward the far end of the closet.
She can barely see anything around her.
Reaching out, she feels her arms and her feet until a moist sensation causes her to retract her hands.
Water is beginning to seep inside!
She tries to open the door, but the door won't budge.

ALISA

SAGE!

The water is filling up faster and Alisa struggles to get out the closet.

ALISA

Sage! Please! Don't do this. Help, please! Someone help me!

She fights with the door until the water reaches the top and Alisa is sucked underwater.
She thrashes around until she sees herself floating in the water.
She touches her own flesh,
A bright light shines above them and a piercing cry stings her ears.
Her own eyes pop open and for a moment she finds herself thrashing in the water.
A few scientists grab her body and try to assist her.
With a plunge of a needle, she is sedated, which pushes her back into her reverie.

The pain of choking up water awakens Alisa, She realizes that there are a few people around, her staring at her.

The Officer with the cool shades on is suspended over her as her vision starts to clear.

OFFICER

I knew I had to keep my eye on you.

ALISA

Where am I?

OFFICER

You're at the Lake. You went out to far, looks like, caught you just in time before you went under.

ALISA

Thank you.

OFFICER

That's what we're here for. We have to look out for you.

Alisa looks at her surroundings, trying to make sense of what just happened.

OFFICER

Is everything ok?

ALISA

Yes, I'm fine. The cure worked...No one's sick.

OFFICER

Maybe I should take you home.

ALISA

No, I'm fine... I need to find Robin.

Fare Corps illuminates in the background as Alisa establishes her path to the structure.

Alisa gains momentum once she nears the building.
She pushes against the solid metal doors leading straight into the lab.
She continues walking by a few scientists, who are doing experiments on all types of creatures that are whining.
The sadist torture disturbs her,
Directing her away from it into a secluded lab room.
She opens the door to reveal Robin and Dr. Fare engaging in a passionate kiss.
. *Horrified, Alisa back up and tries to cover her disbelief.*

ALISA

Daddy? Robin? No.

FATHER

Alisa, it's not what it looks like.

ALISA

Robin, how could you?

ROBIN

I'm so sorry, I didn't want you to find out this way.

ALISA

You're sick.

Alisa leaves the room in a rage.
Tears streaming down her cheeks in panic.
She rushes out the door with Robin calling after her.

CHAPTER TWENTY- TWO

ROBIN GOES LUCID

Jeff helps Robin get situated in a Pod in order to initiate a lucid session.

The chilly water sends shivers down Robin's spine as she is submerged.

Jeff feeds a line through Robin's body as she places a line into his flesh.

Once hooked up to their Pods, Jeff lays down in his Pod, beside Robin.

After he sets his watch, he plugs in his earphones, turns on his tape recording of binaural beats, and then he turns toward Robin.

JEFF

We'll need this, just in case. These will help us reach maximum lucidity.

Jeff holds out a small red pill.

Reluctantly, she takes it.

ROBIN

Now what?

JEFF

Ok, I just need you to breathe. The next thing you remember, you will be in a dream. I want you to pause there for a moment. Wait for me. I will come and find you. Ok?

ROBIN

I'm ready.

JEFF

Ok, let your mind drift. Think of the place where we first met; we'll meet there. In the conference room. Think of meeting me there.

ROBIN

Ok. I'll see you soon.

They both pop the small round pill in their mouths.
The doors on the Pods lock in place, and,
Within a few moments, Robin closes her eyes and lets her mind wander.
She imagines sitting alone in the conference room.
She looks around the walls, then notices there are files all over the table showing Alisa's battered body.
She grabs some of the papers and looks at them.
All of them are the same picture of a vial of blood.
There are also white rats running around her feet.
The door opens, revealing Jeff.

ROBIN

Jeffrey.

JEFF

Robin, listen to me. I know this won't seem real to you, but you're dreaming. None of this is real. I've come to find you and bring you to Alisa.

ROBIN

No...no, I don't know what you are talking about.

The world starts to shake and she looks back over to the table and all the photos are gone. They are now standing back in the lab.
Robin looks over to the Pod and sees Alisa's body floating inside.
Her eyes glide over to her own body and Jeff's body floating in their Pods.

ROBIN

How is this even possible?

JEFF

You're having an out-of-body body experience right now.

ROBIN

What am I?

JEFF

More than we will ever possibly know.

ROBIN

Can I ... communicate with myself?

JEFF

I don't see why we can't. I've never tried.

Robin walks over to her body and finds herself trying to touch herself.

Her body jerks a bit when she gets close.
She's in Reverie.

ROBIN

My god...I'm dreaming.

JEFF

Amazing isn't it? And we don't even know the depths of it yet.

ROBIN

Where's Alisa?

JEFF

Where Alisa always is in my world. Come.

Jeff leads Robin out deeper into the heart of Reverie.

Alisa's world is frigid and cold.

She walks along the path in an uncertain dark world. People pass by her, staring at her, and a few beggars approach begging for money.

She picks up her walking speed and covers her ears until she bumps into someone.

ALISA

I'm sorry.

JEFF

Alisa! Thank God it's you.

ALISA

Jeff?

JEFF

You're ok. Hey, listen, I gave Robin your message.

ALISA

You did?

JEFF

Yea, she was worried about you. She wanted to give you a message back.

ALISA

(surprised)

Oh?

JEFF

Well, we thought it would be better if she would tell you herself.

Jeff steps back to reveal Robin.

ROBIN

Alisa, it's really you!

Alisa face drops and she backs away from her.

ALISA

Get away from me.

ROBIN

Alisa, what's going on? What's wrong?

ALISA

You're disgusting, I don't want anything to do with you!

ROBIN

Alisa, what are you talking about?

ALISA

You lied to me my whole life! And I know why, you were controlling my father.

ROBIN

What? Alisa, that's absurd I would never...Alisa, that memory wasn't real. That didn't happen, your brain created that image of me. You have to believe me.

ALISA

How do I know what you're saying to me now isn't real?

ROBIN

(looks to Jeff)

I don't think she knows she's dreaming. Something happened.

JEFF

Alisa, you're on a mission. You have to kill Sage.

ALISA

No, Sage is my friend...He's helped me.

ROBIN

Alisa, this isn't real. You're dreaming. We sedated you to go on a mission.

(to Jeff)

Show her, Jeff.

JEFF

I'll need help. I haven't interacted with 3 Realities before. Think of the lab.

Robin, Jeff, and Alisa all show up together at the lab, above the bodies of themselves underwater in the Pods.

Alisa spots herself, and she touches the glass of her Pod, searching for meaning.

ALISA

(realizing)

I'm dreaming. This is all a dream.

ROBIN

Shh. It's ok Alisa, it's hard, I know, to determine what's real and what's not.

ALISA

How long have I been sedated?

ROBIN

It's been a couple of days.

ALISA

It feels like eternity in here. How is my body responding to the Virus?

ROBIN

Good, at first. You just entered Phase 4 before we came.

ALISA

Phase 4. What does that mean?

ROBIN

It means that you're progressively getting worse. But, we haven't given up hope. Your Virus is still running its course. We just need to see if your resistance holds it steady. Remember Alisa, it's mind over matter. You can will anything to happen and it will.

ALISA

Not if I lose my mind.

JEFF

So, what are we going to do about Sage?

ALISA

I don't know where he is. I can hardly keep up with him. He told me he loved me.

ROBIN

Alisa, what do you mean?

ALISA

I mean, it's found some sort of attraction to me in some way. He was protecting me from my mind, though he was the cause of my mind attacking itself. I'm still trying to understand it all.

ROBIN

Have you been close at all to try to get rid of him?

ALISA

No, see, that's just it. I don't think I'm meant to kill Sage. Sage isn't a parasite or a bacteria, you can't just get rid of it with a dose of antibiotics. Sage is a Virus, and viruses aren't mean to be eliminated from the body. Instead, they are meant to be suppressed. I think I was looking at the problem all wrong. I think instead of trying to kill Sage, I need to find a way to suppress him.

ROBIN

You've personified Sage? Your mind's projection of the Virus in your brain?

ALISA

I guess so.

ROBIN

What can I do to help you?

ALISA

Nothing. There isn't anything you two can do to help me. Only I can see Sage. Only I can use my mind to suppress him.

(to Robin)

Keep my body safe.

(to Jeff)

Thank you, Jeff.

JEFF

I can't wait till you get out of this place.

The group takes a moment to take in the room before them, their bodies completely sedated and yet their minds fully alive and functioning.

Robin and Jeff walk over to their former selves and begin to whisper in their ears to wake up.

Alisa watches them as they awaken back in Reality, and she stands in the room as they wake up.

ROBIN

Do you think she's still there?

JEFF

If I know her, yes.

Alisa wants to reach out to Robin but resists, heading out the door and back into Reverie.

Whether Robin had been with her father or not,

And no one should ever have to be alone.

Ever.

ROBIN

Did you see that?

A light flashes before them and then slowly dissipates into nothing.

JEFF

She's gone.

ROBIN

I can't believe it.

CHAPTER TWENTY-THREE

CONFRONTATION

A hallway appears in front of Alisa as she mindless ponders around the lost city.

She continues along the long, narrow pathway until she finds herself inside an auditorium.

A podium lights up, shining a spotlight on her.
There is a huge crowd staring up at her, waiting for her to make a speech.

Everyone freezes.

DR. HAGGARD

Ah, Alisa, nice of you to join us this evening. We would like for you to tell us about all your great accomplishments and what you plan on doing for your future goals. Go on, don't be shy, the World awaits.

Everyone unfreezes and Alisa stares above the crowd.
She looks around and her heartbeat pounds in loud waves around her.

ALISA

I..uh....well...I don't have any plans yet.

The crowd gasps and there is some chatter.
A few people are laughing.

ALISA

I want to create a legacy.

SOCIETY
(whispers)

Boo, Boring, What is she talking about?

ALISA

I'm sorry, I can't do this.

Alisa runs off the stage and more people are laughing and growing uneasy.

Alisa runs through the backstage until she gets to a long corridor with a door slowly closing shut at the end.

She runs as fast as she can to the sliding door and barely makes it under in time.

She stands up in an elevator with a group of strangers going slowly up and stopping at every floor.

Alisa is extremely cramped.

Claustrophobic.

As if air is slowly being sucked from the room.

ALISA

Please let me get off here...Excuse me. Please. I need to get off. Wait!

Finally, Alisa manages to get off the elevator and she bolts down the hallway.

She hears faint elevator music playing through the walls and it gets louder as she runs closer to it.

Spiders begin to crawl through cracks in the floor and her whole world begins to tumble.

ALISA

SAGE! Where are you? Please! Help me!

Dr. Haggard comes up from behind her and shoves her against a wall, causing her to fall to the ground as he holds a blade to her throat.

DR. HAGGARD

Sage won't be able to help you anymore. You've betrayed him. You're headed to complete darkness.

Dr. Haggard opens his mouth widely to suck the remaining life out of Alisa until Sage appears and grabs Dr. Haggard off her.

Alisa falls to the ground grabbing her throat, coughing up bits of razors.

She pulls herself up but they are gone.
She is alone in a room made of glass.

Alisa bangs her fists against the wall and then realizes that people don't notice her.

She cries out in agony, pounding angrily at the glass walls.
She hits so hard that her fists begin to bleed but she keeps going.

A couple of people passing by begin to notice her, yet do nothing but point and stare.

She sees the Officer and his team running toward her.

Alisa has a brief moment of relief thinking that they want to help her, but instead they aim their guns at her, waiting for the walls to break open!

The wall begins to crack open but Alisa stops beating on the walls.

She falls to a fetal position and waits until the walls crack around her.

The Officer holds his hands high as he is about to give the command to fire,

Crack, within a second, everything changes.*
Alisa falls through the ground.

Black out-
Till we see rooftops.

Sage is standing on the edge facing away from Alisa.
She picks herself up off the ground, bruised, and bloody.

Sage is dangling by the edge.
She limps toward him, and she is restless.

ALISA

So you're going to jump, Sage?

(pause)

You won't die.

SAGE

It's not about death, Alisa; it never was.

ALISA

Then what is it about huh? Me losing my sanity?

SAGE

I only wanted you to choose.

ALISA

Choose? Choose what?

Alisa looks over to see what Sage is looking at. She sees herself holding onto her dead father, drenching herself in his brain tissue, crying and rocking him.

ALISA

Why are you showing me that?

SAGE

Choose.

ALISA

Choose what, I don't understand what you want me to choose?

SAGE

I love you, Alisa.

ALISA

No, I can't, I can't stay here with you. I have a mission. They never turned their backs on me...they love me!

SAGE

You still can't see.

Alisa looks back over, and she sees herself as a child walking into the living room.

She watches her father as he's having a nervous breakdown. He paces back and forth and it looks like he's on the phone with someone.

DR. FARE

I just didn't think it would take this long to reverse the effects of the Virus. It was supposed to help us, not hurt us. Alisa is reacting normally to the strand. I don't know how it got leaked. Are you sure no one else had access to those cabinets? I have to make this right.

(pause)

No, the dreams and visions are getting worse. I can't stop thinking about hurting her. I feel disgusting for staying this. How can I calm down? I want to kill my own child. I don't want to hurt anyone else. I have to go.

Dr. Fare paces around and then he picks up a gun from off the counter.

DR. FARE

I can't...I can't...But I have to...for her safety. There's no need in saving them...it's done. Just finish the job.

A little Alisa comes down the stairs.

ALISA

Daddy?

Dr. Fare points the gun at the young Alisa and his hand is shaking.

FATHER

I'm sorry baby. For everything. It's you.

Dr. Fare pulls the trigger on himself and he falls to the ground.

Alisa cries out as she drops beside him, covering herself in his blood.

Sage is standing on the rooftop still waiting for Alisa. She is shaking with anger.

ALISA

Why would my father want me to choose you? You killed him.

SAGE

I saved your life.

ALISA

No, no. I won't listen to you anymore. I choose my family. Humanity. Hope. My father was crazy. He didn't know what he was talking about. It was because of you—you drove him mad!

Alisa inches Sage closer to the edge.

ALISA

Tell me Sage, ever wonder what it's like to find a self-destructing Virus? I can't kill you, but maybe a virus can infect its own self. Let's see how long you can fall.

SAGE

I'd do anything for you, Alisa.

Alisa's face softens and she finds herself trying to stop herself from pushing him.

He inches off himself,

which makes him fall off the building.

Sage slowly touches her face one last time as he descends.

She looks over the edge and he's no longer there.

The sun shines through the clouds letting the light brighten her Reverie.

CHAPTER TWENTY-FOUR

IS IT REALITY?

Reality isn't always as it presents itself.
She cleans up well, but that's only on the outside.

The inside of her will eat you alive; but it's just her nature, how could you ever question that?

Robin never has. She carefully checks on the blinking stats on Alisa's EKG monitor.

Her breathing is steady, and her brain activity seems constant, until a surge of light pulses across the screen showing a drop in brain function.

Alisa's vital signs plummet and her heart stops beating, alerting a flat-line on the screen.

The machines all start going off in panic.

ROBIN
Hey, hey, hey, what's going on, what's happening?

Jeff hops up out of his chair to help pull Alisa out of her Pod.

JEFF
Don't worry. I know what I'm doing.

ROBIN
What's happening, I don't understand, she was just in Phase 4...I've never seen anyone drop so suddenly!

JEFF
She's not in Phase 4, she's in Phase 5. Get her out of the tank now. Bring me the defibrillators.

They pull Alisa out of the tank and place her on a patient bed.

Robin brings the defibrillators over to him and he begins to prep them.

JEFF

Ok, on my count, one, two, three.

Jeff zaps Alisa.

Alisa is out in a wide field under the beautiful open skies. She dances around in a flowing gown and in the distance she sees a bright white light.

ALISA

Wow. I've never seen something so beautiful.

Alisa is drawn toward the light until there is a loud buzz of lighting across the sky.

Alisa looks off in the other direction and sees darkness seeping through.

ALISA

No. No, I'm coming.

VOICE

(gentle)

Alisa.

ALISA

It's you.

VOICE

It's not time.

ALISA

What? No, I'm ready.

VOICE

They need you.

ALISA

No. No one needs me. I need you.

VOICE

In time. In time....

The Voice fades and another lightning bolt strikes across the sky.

Dark clouds begin to set in as the light slowly goes away. Alisa loses her balance, bringing her to the ground.

ALISA

No! Not yet, please. Please don't go! NO!

Alisa is sucked back into Reality.
She opens her eyes and everything is blurry.
Looking around the room, she is disorientated.

ROBIN

Alisa, thank God!

ALISA
(slurring)

No! No.

Robin pulls away to give Alisa some room to breathe and she sits there for a moment, blinking her eyes slowly.

ROBIN

She's been in a sedated state for a while. I think she needs some space. Please.

A few people leave the room, except for Robin and Jeff.

Alisa closes her eyes and then quietly lies there, shaking her head.
Robin grabs a nearby water bottle and gelatin cup.
She holds them out to Alisa, hoping it may help bring her peace.
Alisa rises up, eying the two before her.

ROBIN

So glad to see you have some strength to pull yourself up. Feeling any better?

ALISA
(shaking head)

No.

ROBIN

It may take some time.

ALISA

Why couldn't you just leave me there?

ROBIN

What?

ALISA

I was happy, peaceful, it's where I belong. I felt it.

ROBIN

Alisa, we were losing you. You were dying.

ALISA

I saw a light.

ROBIN

I've heard that's what you see close to that time.

ALISA

It was the most beautiful thing I've ever seen. I was home.

ROBIN

I'm sorry.

ALISA

Sage is gone.

ROBIN

No. You suppressed him; he's still there.

ALISA

(shaking her head)

It's different. I don't feel him anymore.

ROBIN

You took control, you did great! This is exactly what we wanted.

ALISA

(hurt)

What now?

ROBIN

We save millions of lives.

They smile at each other and then Jeff approaches them.
Alisa and Jeff make eye contact for the first time in Reality,
Intensely,
As they stare at each other, unsure what to say.

ROBIN

Well, uhm, I'm glad you're feeling better. I need to get the room ready for your extraction process. Excuse me.

Robin leaves, allowing the two to get reacquainted.

JEFF

Hey Alisa, it's nice to meet you. I'm Jeff.

Alisa moves herself closer to Jeff as she searches his eyes. She reaches out to touch his face but stops herself when he removes a small strand of her hair from her cheek.

ALISA

Hi. It's nice to meet you too.

JEFF

I know this all seems surreal, but I promise you, it was all real to me— every feeling, everything. I was there and I'll always be there. One step at a time, ok?

ALISA

(nodding)

Ok.

After a moment of sweet remembrance, the door slams open and Robin enters.

ROBIN

Sorry to interrupt but we're having a few issues at the entrance. It seems that we've had a breach in the West Wing and we have some Ailings that have gotten inside. Mostly Phase 5's, violent and dangerous. I'm going to need to get you somewhere safe so we can continue with the extraction process.

Alisa follows Robin out the door and down a narrow hallway to a more secure location.

A few scientists are trying to regulate the Ailings, but they are pushing and attacking any one in their way.

Alisa and Jeff follow Robin along the corridor until they reach a locked door.

Robin bangs on the door, but it's useless.

ROBIN

Oh no. Ok, we'll try the side entrance.

They run back around to where they came from, and into a gruesome scene.

A pool of blood lines the floor along with flickering lights and dead mangled bodies.

Alisa's can't tear her eyes off the mutated corpses while Robin seeks for other options.

Jeff pulls out a Taser from his jeans pocket and holds it in front of him.

ALISA

Where did you get that?

JEFF

Safety first, especially during these times.

Robin starts breaking open a door that has been wedged shut in the back corner of the room.

She cracks open the window with a metal bar she finds laying near the pool of blood.

There are a couple of Phase 5's that sense their presence as they come bolting down the hallway, straight at them.

Once they all get inside the new room, they quickly shut the door, just in time to barricade themselves in.

The room they've shut themselves in is in shambles. Alisa notices the blood splattered on all the walls.

As they get further into the room they take notice of a few dead scientists laying around the room, torn to shreds.

ALISA

Are you sure this is a good spot?

ROBIN

Yes, it'll do for now.

Robin takes out her supplies and she sets them all out on a dusty table.

ALISA

I think it's better if we just leave the facility. My father's lab would be perfect for this sort of thing; he's got so much equipment there to make it for the best place for disbursement.

Robin ties up Alisa's arm with an elastic band and Jeff watches the door.

Alisa flinches in pain as Robin sticks a thin needle into her soft vein that is protruding from the light slap Robin gives her to help it rise.

ALISA

How much blood do you think you'll need to take?

Jeff and Alisa watch as Robin extracts the blood from Alisa's arm.

The clear plasma quickly fills the tube,
Jeff's eyebrows rise.
Clear blood?
What is she?
She wasn't human after all.

ROBIN

It's important to find out now, before we go anywhere, if we've really found the cure or not.

ALISA

But, I'm alive Robin, of course we've found a cure!

ROBIN

I'll be the first to really tell you if we have or not.

JEFF

No, no wait a minute, what's going on here? What is this?

Robin plunges herself with Alisa's blood into her own body and they watch her intensely, waiting for a reaction.

ALISA

(gasping)

Robin.

Robin steps back for a moment and then she staggers back into a shelf.

Alisa stands up to aid her.

ALISA

Robin, are you ok? How do you feel?

ROBIN

I feel...I feel...great.

Alisa embraces Robin with relief.

Jeff coughs in anticipation for his own shot,

Disregarding the questions streaming through his mind,

He is going to be well again.

JEFF

(shocking)

My God, it works. Well, I'm in Phase 4, let's do something before I lose my mind.

Robin gathers another vial of blood from Alisa.

Once the blood fills the syringe she takes it over to Jeff as he rolls up his sleeves.

She wraps the strap around his arm allowing his veins to pop up to the surface.

JEFF

We did it! We saved humanity.

Robin lowers the needle.

BANG!

The Ailings are trying to get in!

Robin freezes in place, her eyes start reddening and her nose seeps blood down her face.

ALISA

Robin…your nose.

Robin drops the needle and begins to throw up all over the room, grabbing onto the table before falling over.

Jeff grabs Alisa and holds up his taser to Robin.

ALISA

Jeff, what are you doing? She needs help.

JEFF

No Alisa, she's entering Phase 5.

Alisa waits as Robin slowly claws her way up to a standing position.

Robin's eyes are glazed over and she hisses at them.

Robin charges at them and Jeff pulls out the taser and fires it at her.

Robin falls to the ground and Alisa cries out for her.

ALISA

(sobbing)

Robin! No! no.

JEFF

(serious)

Do you know your way around this facility?

ALISA

A few ways, I don't remember.

JEFF

You have to try.

They think for a moment until they hear some moaning coming from the closet next to them.

Jeff goes to investigate. He pulls open the door to reveal Ethan.

He is barely breathing.

ALISA

(panic)

Ethan, my god! You're going to be ok…it's going to be ok!

Alisa kneels down beside him and he wheezes.

She touches his face to try to clear a pathway for him to breathe, but he's already lost a lot of blood.

ETHAN

She got away. I tried to stop her.

ALISA

What are you talking about?

ETHAN

She said Robin was the leak, Robin wouldn't do this to us....She would never...

ALISA

Shh, shh, it doesn't matter. It's going to be ok.

JEFF

Alisa, we have to hurry, we don't have much time.

Jeff finds a door, which is slowly caving in by crazed Ailings.

ALISA

Ethan, you're a strong man. You always have been.

(pause; heavy breathing)

Listen, we have to get out of this place...Are there any other exits we can take?

ETHAN

(quietly)

Yes.

Ethan points to a vent across the room.

ALISA

The tunnels! It's for safety measures. Around the corner.

JEFF

Ok, let's go.

ALISA

Wait, we can't just leave him here to die like this.

ETHAN

(weakly)

Alisa, you have to go. Please. We've come too far now. Go!

ALISA

I won't leave you, Ethan!

ETHAN

I'm sorry for everything they put you through. You're a lovely girl Alisa. I hope you get all of your memory back.

Alisa is confused by the words that Ethan is saying to her.

Jeff looks back at the door, which is now almost halfway open. Ethan slowly dies in Alisa's arms,

She won't let go until Jeff pries her from him. He picks her up and runs with her to find the exit.

She squirms and kicks, crying out Ethan's name. He finally puts her down once he spots the small opening near the floor.

He pulls off the screen and backs away so that Alisa can lead them into the tunnel.

She looks at him with tear stained eyes that rip deep into his soul, and there isn't anything he can do about it.

They crawl through the muddy tunnels, leaving Alisa deep in thought until Jeff breaks the silence.

JEFF

What was he talking about? She got away? Who got away?

ALISA

(upset)

I don't know. He sounded delirious; I don't know if he even knew what he was talking about.

(pause)

I thought we found a cure.

JEFF

I did too.

ALISA

But my blood made it worse.

JEFF

That's not blood that runs through your veins…

(pause)

Maybe the virus damaged too much of her brain.

ALISA

You mean there could still be a chance?

JEFF

You have resistance to the Virus. Your DNA means something. We just need to test it.

ALISA

Who, Jeff?

JEFF

We'll find a way.

Alisa keeps crawling until they finally see the light at the end of the tunnel.

She reaches the end, but there are bars blocking their exit. Alisa struggles to break them open, then she begins to kick them with her feet.

Once the bars are loose they are able to crawl to a city falling into ruins.

JEFF

Come on, we're on foot.

Alisa follows Jeff toward the outskirts of the roads.

Her eyes flow over the sick and the madness arising all around her.

Screams pierce her ears as the Ailings attack their own selves. What is this insanity?

They find a few abandoned cars with keys still inside.

None of the car have gas. Jeff finally finds one that works and they get in and take off.

Contemplation takes over Alisa's mind as they drift across the lonely roads before them.

She rubs her head, taken back by the new world she's in.

ALISA

This is...our world?

JEFF

Isn't she lovely? Well, before people got to her.

ALISA

I don't understand. Nothing in Reverie looked like this.

JEFF

Welcome to Reality.

ALISA

This is what we're trying to save?

JEFF

Hey, hey, we're not so bad.

ALISA

I'm just trying to understand it, that's all.

JEFF

We're just humans. Trying to make it—working, saving lives, helping others, loving each other.

ALISA

I've seen.

JEFF

But you haven't experienced. This won't be a great experience for you. This isn't who we are.

ALISA

I know. My father gave everything to try to protect us.

JEFF

And he did well.

The gas light comes on.

Jeff groans, but notices a gas station coming up on his right.

JEFF

You can wait here, I'll just be a minute, we need some gas. Want anything?

ALISA

Actually...yes. I'll get it, I need to stretch my legs anyway.

JEFF

Ok.

Alisa hops out the car and goes into the shop.

It looks abandoned at first; but then she sees someone behind the counter with his back facing away from her.

She searches the candy aisle looking for a quick treat.

A paper rack catches her eyes,

She picks up the paper and scans for the date.

Nov. 12. 2111.

She nearly drops the paper, gasping.

2111.

"S.A.G.E EPIDEMIC" is painted across the front page along with a picture of her father, Robin, and the team.

She continues to read the paper about technology's new advancements and how the public has turned in on itself.

She closes the paper, brings it to the counter along with a candy bar, and as she reaches for her Chip the young guy turns around.

It's Ethan.

ETHAN

Alisa, long time no see.

ALISA
(shocked)
Ethan. No...it can't be...you're…dead.

ETHAN
Don't be silly Alisa, I'm right here.

ALISA
Sage?

ETHAN
Sage? Are you ok, Alisa? Are you saying you're dreaming?

ALISA
No...I'm...Is this a dream? Am I dreaming?

Jeff looks into the gas station and is worried about Alisa. She's taking longer than he thought.

He places the gas pump back in its place and walks toward the entrance to see her standing at the counter talking to herself.

ETHAN
(dark)
Alisa.

ALISA
(stops flatly; scared)
Ethan?

Ethan transforms into Sage before her eyes.

ALISA
(mortified)
Why are you doing this?

SAGE

Because nothing is what it seems.

ALISA

What did you do to my head?

SAGE

The mind is so fragile.

ALISA

No, I won't listen to you any longer, you're gone!

JEFF

Alisa?

Alisa realizes Jeff is close to her, she checks for Ethan, but Ethan is gone.

ALISA

I...I thought someone was here.

JEFF

Who?

ALISA

No one. It's ok. Let's go.

They both exit the shop with a few snacks in their hands. Alisa takes a second look into the window to see Ethan once more, waving at her.

She closes her eyes,

Hoping to push him far back with her other repressed memories.

Back on the road,
Alisa is slowly falling in and out of sleep but she forces herself to stay awake.

JEFF

You should rest.

ALISA

I'm fine.

JEFF

I wish I could rest.

ALISA

Do you want me to drive?

JEFF

You can drive?

ALISA

No. But it doesn't look that hard. Press on the gas and steer right? Try to stay in between the lines?

JEFF

Sure.

ALISA

I guess that's a no.

JEFF

You haven't touched any of your food.

ALISA

I'm not hungry.

Jeff gives her a look of worry.

ALISA

Fine.

She opens a bag of chips and takes a bite.

It slowly melts onto her tongue and her eyes relax.
She realizes how much she's missed food.
Jeff periodically checks on her as she devours the rest of her food.
This helps to settle him.

JEFF
Slow down. I don't think you can eat the bag.

ALISA
That was the best bag of chips I ever had in my entire life.

JEFF
Wow, you need to get out more.

Alisa sticks her tongue out.
They keep driving until they get to a familiar neighborhood.

JEFF
Does this ring a bell to you?

ALISA
(peering out the window)
It does. Why are we over here?

JEFF
I'm just showing you...all the places we visited in our dreams.

ALISA
Is our special place real?

JEFF
What do you mean?

ALISA
The place you would always bring me to, with the bridge overlooking the pond?

JEFF

It's not. There's no place like it here in the city. I guess I—we created it.

(pause)

That's why it's so special.

(pause)

So, we know that your blood doesn't react well to Phase 3 and I'm assuming Phase 4. We need to test it on a Phase 2 patient…and I know just where to go.

CHAPTER TWENTY-FIVE

CLINIC

Jeff enters the hospital with Alisa. They try to avoid some of the Ailings who try to grab at them and are hostile.

They get Dr. Thompkins office. He is inside looking over some papers.

DR. THOMPKINS

Ah, Jeffrey, and you've brought a friend!

JEFF

We've found a cure.

DR. THOMPKINS

(peaking interest)

You don't say!

JEFF

Its classified information and we've only tested it on one person so far, which didn't end up with the best results. However, due to the fact you are only in Phase 2 of the Virus, we think you might benefit greatly...and even be cured.

DR. THOMPKINS

And this young lady is?

JEFF

Is the cure.

DR. THOMPKINS

(laughing as if it's absurd)

What Phase are you in, dear?

ALISA

I am not in any Phase, sir. My antibodies have build up a resistance to the Virus, leaving me with full resistance.

DR. THOMPKINS

(passive)

Unbelievable.

JEFF

Sir, we need to know. And I know how badly you want this.

Dr. Thompkins thinks for a moment, but then he looks at how healthy and vibrant Alisa is.

DR. THOMPKINS

I can't. I moved to Phase 3 earlier this morning. The Virus moves too quickly. I don't think we have anyone left in Phase 2 in the whole clinic.

Alisa and Jeff look at each other in disappointment.

JEFF

No one? We're too late.

ALISA

I'm sorry Jeff…

DR. THOMPKINS

I told you to go home, Jeffrey, this is no place for you right now, you need to be home. I'll be leaving soon; I just have one last patient to see. Ok? Can you do just this one last thing for an old man like me?

Jeff nods his head, leaving Dr. Thompkins's weary hands to continue to work on prescriptions that would never be filled.

The two leave the clinic with unanswered questions and a hole in their hearts.

They continue along a dirt path until they find themselves entering a neighborhood.

A Mill tent is set up at the entrance enticing the sick and Ailings to eat if they are hungry.

Jeff spots his old friend from the rest of the Givers. Her warm smile comforts his swollen spirit.

KEELY

Jeff!

(she runs over to him, embracing him)

You're back, are you feeling any better?

JEFF

(lying)

A little. I've gotten rest. How are you holding up?

KEELY

I'm doing my best. Better than the other Givers at this Mill. I haven't hit Phase 3 yet so I always say that's a positive sign. Good genes, I guess.

JEFF

Phase 2?

KEELY

Yes, just hit it a few days ago.

JEFF

Keely, how would you like to be 100% healthy again?

KEELY

That would be the best gift ever. That would mean there is hope. We haven't had hope in a very long time.

JEFF

We'll we're about to give you that hope. We've found a cure.

KEELY

A cure?

JEFF

Yea. All you have to do is sit back and get better.

KEELY

I don't understand.

Keely finally notices Alisa as she steps forward.

ALISA

We think your body might still have a fighting chance against the Virus. It hasn't seeped too far into the core of your brain.

Keely's eyes sweep over Alisa's warm face and her thick black hair that drapes over her shoulders.

KEELY

What phase are you in? You look so great.

ALISA

I've achieved full resistance, and you can too.

Keely looks back and forth at both of them, she speaks quietly.

KEELY

Ok, follow me.

Keely leads them into a wooded area near the neighborhood park to prepare her for the injection.

She holds out her arms and Alisa grabs a vial from her backpack and gets it ready for injection.

JEFF

Are you ready?

ALISA

Take a deep breath, and it'll all be over.

KEELY

And what happens if it doesn't work out?

Jeff reveals his taser to Alisa, unknown to Keely.

ALISA

Then, I guarantee you will still be happy and healthy. Either way you will be free from this Virus.

KEELY

Ok. Let's do it.

Jeff quickly injects the cure into her arm and then they wait a moment.

Keely rubs the site of the injection, they all hold their breaths, hoping, waiting, expecting.

KEELY

It stings a little.

Keely gets up feeling a little dizzy.

ALISA

Hey, take it easy, maybe you should lie down?

Keely sits back down,and
Alisa rubs her back while Keely begins to gag.

She throws up on the ground, and as she lifts her head back up Jeff draws his taser.

KEELY
(scared)

What are you doing?

Alisa examines Keely's eyes and realizes she is actually accepting the drug.

ALISA

How are you feeling?

KEELY

A little better. A little nauseous. dizzy. Are these the usual side effects?

ALISA

Looks like there might be some.

KEELY

Does this mean I'm cured?

ALISA

We won't know for sure, give it a couple of days...I would go home and rest it off.

KEELY

Thank you so much. I really believe I've been cured. I feel different, clear headed.

Jeff and Alisa cautiously watch her as she pulls her sleeves back down.

KEELY

How's Dr. Thompkins holding up? Did you tell him what you found?

JEFF

Yea we stopped by him first. He's moving too rapidly to Phase 4. I don't think he's going to be coming home any time soon. It's probably best for him.

KEELY

What about what's best for you? Are you going home?

Jeff makes eye contact with Alisa, and he realizes he is home.

JEFF

I think I'll be fine.

Keely maintains her composure as she lowers her head to him.

KEELY

Be well Jeff, I hope this isn't the last time we see each other, and if it is, I want you to have this.

She hands him her brown bag with an emblem of a hawk on the outside.

JEFF

Keely, I can't take this…

KEELY

Sure you can, it's got everything you could ever need. Someone has to take care of you when I'm not around. I'm sure she'll be great.

Keely winks at Alisa before holding up her hand to salute them, bidding her farewell.

Alisa scans over Jeff's face as he watches Keely walk back toward the Mill tent.

ALISA

Do you think it worked?

JEFF

We'll follow up. But, I think we've made progress. Now, it's time to make it for the masses.

The neighborhood begins to take shape as she takes a closer look.

A large lamppost directs her attention to the time on the clock, 11:11.

She follows the direction of the clock as it faces a house toward the back of the street.

It's her neighborhood.
Her house is near.

She can feel the "click clock" chime along with the clock in her own self.

Call it fate. Call it destiny,
She is home.

CHAPTER TWENTY- SIX

HOME

Home is not always where the heart is.
And whoever came up with that saying, is well, in fact, wrong.

Home, Alisa comes to believe, is a place where she feels the most at peace.

And that's was, strangely, in the eyes of Sage.
So when Alisa steps up the stairs to peer into her darkened old house, she realizes how little she really knows about the life she lived before entering the Pod.

Jeff tries the door but it's locked.
Alisa, feeling spontaneous, and having no personal ties with the house, grabs a rock and throws it through the window.

JEFF
(sarcastic)
Ok, so we didn't want to try looking for a spare?

ALISA
No. We didn't keep spares...but there's always a way in, isn't there?

They step through the shattered glass into the living room.

ALISA
(whispers to herself)
Just as he left it. Just like in Reverie.

JEFF
You never let me come in here.

ALISA
What?

JEFF

You always stopped me at the door. Never cut on any lights. Kept this place a secret.

ALISA

It's not a great place to be.

JEFF

Where's this lab?

ALISA

Right this way.

Alisa opens a door leading down to the basement area to a secret door.

Jeff follows Alisa down into the darkness.

Alisa opens up another door to a whole other research room filled with bright lights, with all kinds of instruments and papers scattered along the tables.

ALISA

My dad stayed down here for hours, days even. I can remember practically begging him to feed me when he would get into his research studies. It was always going to be a new day, and he just needed more time.

JEFF

That's dedication.

ALISA

Dedication? Or aAddiction? Robin didn't tell me much about the S.A.G.E. She just kept feeding me this talk about being the cure. I always wanted to know where it came from.

JEFF

I guess you could never watch the news, huh?

ALISA

It was on the news?

JEFF

Yea, it was all over the news. Front page news, magazines. The Internet. The S.A.G.E Epidemic. A violent Virus outbreak from Fare Corps. They didn't know where exactly the leak came from but it had to be someone who had access to these files. The Virus was meant to be used to create a new type of superhuman of evolved consciousness. However, it was shown to have adverse effects on us, attacking our minds and bringing out our own evil desires on ourselves and others.

(pause)

The Virus was meant to basically weed out the weak and to evolve the younger generations to achieve immunity and a new awareness of themselves. But even with that there was an adverse effect. The mind began to reject the body and the physical realm. The higher consciousness is too complex for a simple physical plane. And that's where Sage keeps you, within your own mind.

Alisa is scanning over files and she finally picks up some papers and her face goes pale.

ALISA

My father was the leak.

JEFF

What?

ALISA

It all makes sense now. The phone call. He was talking to Robin. They were working together.

Alisa reads an article and sees Robin and her father smiling and doing research together. Journal Article: "NEW DISCOVERY – EVOLUTIONARY."

ALISA

He created Sage to stir evolution. But he failed. He knew that we couldn't evolve anymore to a higher consciousness because we'd never want to return back to this place. Our brains were so expanded that physical planes were too simple to comprehend. And the body and mind tried to fix itself by rejecting Sage, and yet it still took over and controlled them, turning people mad.

JEFF

What are we going to do now?

ALISA

There was never a cure for the Virus, Jeff. It's only temporary. The younger the generation the more likely their immune system can suppress the disease. All we can do now is wait, and build a resistance.

LACEY

You forgot a few minor details, Jeff.

JEFF

Lacey!

Lacey steps into the room, very pale and fatigued. She takes a deep breath and holds a gun on both of them.

LACEY

You see, they were weak. They didn't have what it took to hold power. To go through with the best plan there could ever be.

ALISA

Lacey, please. I don't understand.

LACEY

Robin went into the locked cabinet and took out the vial. She did her own experimentation on rodents and she messed up. Her error cost millions of lives.

Lacey clicks on a screen above them and allows video surveillance to play:

Robin takes out a vial of blood from one of the secured cabinets while working late at night in the labs with rodents.

She tries to cover it up when she sees Ethan call out to her. Another scientist goes to grab some of the rodents and cross contamination occurs between the animals.

A scientist accidently scars the infected rodent, which in returns bites him.

Robin captures all the rodents and ends up getting rid of them, thinking she successfully contained the disease. However, it's already been spread to the scientist via his cut.

Lacey still stands in front of Jeff and Alisa barely holding herself together.

Her hand begins to shake.

LACEY

Don't you see? You've been fed so many lies, Alisa. Isn't that right, Jeffrey? You always wanted to help her, didn't you?

Alisa looks at Jeff confused as to what Lacey is talking about.

LACEY

Oh, so you still haven't told her, have you?

JEFF

I don't know what you're talking about Lacey, but clearly your mind is slipping.

LACEY

No, my thoughts are perfectly clear. She needs to know the truth.

JEFF

Lacey, I really don't know what you're talking about. Please, put down the gun and we can talk about this.

LACEY

Alisa, Jeff here has been your neighbor since your father passed away and you were brought into this facility. He's been trying to get you out of Fare Corps ever since you were placed here. He's attempted to see you multiple times causing you to begin acting out; you began to question your free will. We even had a few suicide attempts on behalf of your love for Jeff.

Robin thought it was in your best interest that we find a quick solution to this problem, so we thought it was best if we suppressed most of the memories of you and Jeff. We did the same with Jeff, of course with his agreement. We knew there could be a possibility with the subconscious that Sage would begin to open your mind back up to the possible romance of you two...but, under no circumstance could you know that, in fact, it was a reality.

Jeff looks at Alisa strangely and then turns back to Lacey.

JEFF

You're lying.

LACEY

I wish I was, but she needed to know the truth. I was always on your side, Alisa; it wasn't fair. I made a promise to both of you. I was the only one you trusted in this place.

There is a long, awkward silence and Alisa searches Lacey's face for the truth.

ALISA

I believe you.

Jeff pauses for a moment to look away to think deeply about the whole situation.
He grabs his head in anger.

JEFF
(to Lacey)

I told you to do not to do this!

LACEY

She deserved the truth!

JEFF

Why reveal the ugly truth, when you can live a beautiful lie?

Alisa tries to take it all in,
But it breaks her down.

ALISA
(crying)

What do we do now?

LACEY

Put me out my misery.

Lacey hands Alisa the gun and Alisa stares at her, now her hands are shaky.

ALISA

I can't. I won't.

LACEY

I came here to do what I had to do. To tell you what you needed to know before it was too late. One day you will remember. Now, please. I've done what I've come to do.

For a second Alisa is frozen as she sees Lacey bracing herself for a gunshot.

LACEY

Please Alisa, I'm slipping, I don't want to lose my mind. Don't let me become like one of those animals.

Alisa holds up the gun and Lacey gives a small smile as Alisa closes her eyes, pulling the trigger.

The gun falls to the ground and Lacey collapses. Alisa rushes to catch her but Jeff grabs her.

She notices that Jeff's nose is starting to bleed. He slumps over and she pulls him over to a chair.

He coughs up some blood and his eyes are turning red.

ALISA

Jeff. Jeff. Don't do this to me now?

JEFF

I think it's almost about that time.

ALISA

No Jeff! You can't leave me alone.

JEFF

I can't think clearly anymore.

ALISA

What? Don't talk like that.

JEFF

Alisa, I'm Phase 4, we knew it would be coming. I have to keep you safe.

ALISA

No, we still have a little more time.

JEFF

No, Alisa, we don't. I can feel myself slipping.

ALISA

I...I can...

JEFF

Alisa, I don't want to lose my mind, or hurt you.

Jeff grabs the gun from Alisa and cocks it.

JEFF

I have to do this.

ALISA

No, Jeff. I don't want to be away from you.

JEFF

You won't be. I'll be right here.

(points to her head)

ALISA

What am I going to do here without you?

JEFF
You have everything you need here, gather up the others that are Immune; start a Resistance.

ALISA
No, I can't. I can't do this alone.

JEFF
You can. This is what you were born for. You have to be their light. Make the decisions.

ALISA
Jeff. Please! I can't make decisions now, they've crippled me, I'm damaged. I can't do this on my own.

JEFF
I won't be too far from you. You know where to meet me.
(pause)
I can't do this in front of you.

ALISA
Where are you going to go?

Jeff kisses her on the forehead.

JEFF
Meet me tonight. I love you Alisa.

Jeff climbs back up the stairs of the basement leaving Alisa alone amongst the cluttered papers, the twisted truth.

She thinks for a moment but then she bolts after Jeff who drives away with tears streaming down his face.

ALISA
Jeff, Jeff...please…don't...don't do it... I need you...

The car is too fast for her to catch on foot.
As she watches, the hawk on the license plate get further and further away.
She runs back into the house, into the lab to grab a sedative and she plunges it into her thigh to knock her into Reverie.

In Reverie, Alisa sees Jeff waiting for her next to the pond. He looks at her and smiles.

JEFF

Alisa.

ALISA

Jeff.

Alisa collapses into his arms and she holds him tightly.

ALISA

I don't ever want to leave you.

JEFF

You never have to. I'm here.

ALISA

Jeff, we did it. We are safe here.

JEFF

No Alisa, you have to go back.

ALISA

No, no, I want to stay here with you.

JEFF

There's still something you have to do.

ALISA

What are you talking about? I want to be with you.

JEFF

When's the last time you talked to Sage?

ALISA

Sage...Sage is gone. Suppressed. We never have to worry about him again.

JEFF

You need to find him.

ALISA

What are you saying?

JEFF

This isn't our end goal. I'm sorry Alisa. I thought it was, but I was wrong. I saw the light....and you're right...it's such a beautiful light.

ALISA

Jeff…Jeff…no, don't leave me...you said you would be here...don't leave me...

Jeff begins to fade and Alisa stands in the middle of the bridge, searching.

She runs off into the city, yelling in a rage for Sage.

ALISA

SAGE! Sage! Answer me! I know you're in here. I'm calling you out!

Alisa walks into a white room that appears very glossy. She looks around and sees a young Alisa playing in a dollhouse along with Sage who is kneeling beside her.

ALISA

You were with me. The whole time?

(realizes)

You were Sarah.

SAGE

Alisa.

Sage picks himself up and strolls over next to Alisa.

SAGE

It's ok Alisa, I'll be right back.

YOUNG ALISA

Ok, Sarah, I'll play for you while you're away.

Alisa and Sage walk through an enchanted rose garden with a path painted in gold.

ALISA

Where did you take Jeff? Why did he tell me to come see you? You win, ok! Just give me Jeff back. I choose you, Sage.

SAGE

You won't have Jeff that way.

ALISA

Just bring me Jeff back, I'll do anything.

SAGE

This is not your destination, Alisa.

ALISA

What are you talking about?

SAGE

I only wanted you to see.

ALISA

What? What did you want me to see?!

SAGE

This is Limbo. Your body will slowly cease to exist; in the end you're only killing yourself slowly. This is not your destiny.

ALISA

I just want to be with Jeff. You've taken everything away from me. What more do you want?

SAGE

Choose.

Alisa thinks for a moment but then she has a revelation when she looks back at Alisa playing in the dollhouse.

ALISA

For once, you want me to choose for myself. To make my own decision.

SAGE

You have purpose, Alisa. A human's greatest hope is love and rebirth. Raise a new generation. It's your choice, Alisa. You carry the cure.

Alisa looks back at the child playing in the dollhouse.

ALISA

I choose me.

Sage finally gives her a grim smile and then he begins to fade away.

Alisa stands there until she falls to the ground, where she sees a dandelion budding from the soil.

She grabs the flower and blows it onto the World and we follow the dandelion's dance till we see...

EPILOGUE

A dandelion floats through the air, sweeping Alisa's hair. She remembers Sage as she sits in front of the camp.

A bald middle-aged man greets her at the entrance. He holds out his hand to her.

MAN

Ah, Alisa, we've been waiting for you.

Alisa rises to reveal the alliance of many young children awaiting her arrival.

MAN

Welcome to the Resistance.

Made in the USA
Las Vegas, NV
07 October 2021

31877103R00103